BIGFOOT COP

Also by Kevin Shamel:

Rotten Little Animals

Island of the Super People

BIGFOOT COP

KEVIN SHAMEL

ERASERHEAD PRESS
PORTLAND, OREGON

ERASERHEAD PRESS
205 NE BRYANT STREET
PORTLAND, OR 97211

WWW.ERASERHEADPRESS.COM

ISBN: 978-1-62105-138-1
1-62105-138-2

Printed in the USA.

You cannot go against Nature
Because when you do
Go against Nature,
It's part of Nature, too.

—Love and Rockets

Chapter 1

Bigfoot ate a salad in his unmarked police car. He hated the sedan. Even with the seat all the way back, he had to sit crunched up behind the wheel. His feet didn't fit on the pedals, so he had to use just one toe for the gas. The seatbelt certainly didn't work for him. The laptop mounted on the center console dug into his leg. He pushed against it and broke off one of its welded brackets.

To sit straight in a car was impossible unless it had a sunroof. Like most police vehicles, his did not. The driver's seat would have to be replaced if someone else were to drive it. His head had already dented the roof, and he'd only had the car for three days. He tended to go through them quickly. Bigfoot flicked an olive out the window. It was especially difficult to eat in the car.

A call came over the radio, "Armed robbery in progress, corner of Quimby and 17th Street." It was three blocks away.

Bigfoot threw the salad and growled into his handset, "Bigfooooot!" He started the car, cranked it into gear and stomped his toe on the gas.

He spotted the robbers exiting a warehouse and screeched to a stop in the middle of the road. Bigfoot jumped out of his car, hitting his head on the edge of the door and twisting its frame. His slacks ripped along the seams of his legs and ass as he bounded toward the armed men.

The chief shouted from the radio in the open car,

"Bigfoot, do *not* respond! Bigfoot! Come in, Bigfoot! Ah, godDAMNI—"

The three men aimed pistols and a sawed-off shotgun at Bigfoot. Bullets flew, punching holes in parked cars, ricocheting off walls and pavement, even hitting Bigfoot a few times. There were shouts and screams. People ran into nearby buildings.

Bigfoot went straight to their getaway car and slammed his fist through its hood. He pulled at spinning motor parts until he'd torn the engine off its mount. It screeched to a smoking halt. The windshield exploded in stars of shattered glass as the man inside opened fire with his automatic rifle.

Bigfoot flipped the car over, spinning it through the air and onto the sidewalk across the street and crunching the driver between the flattened roof and car interior. The car bounced over the curb before it crashed through the windows of a printing shop.

White pops of electricity and leaking gasoline sparked a fire in the building. Flames engulfed the car, spreading quickly to mangled office furniture. Smoke billowed from broken windows. Workers ran into the street, some dragging others, some crawling, some falling and limping, everyone shouting and coughing.

Bullets needled Bigfoot's back. He turned, lunged and grabbed the barrel of an assault rifle. Bigfoot pushed the butt of the gun into the shooter's jaw, crushing bone, shattering most of his teeth and snapping his neck.

The robber flew backward into a hulking assailant, who shot at Bigfoot with two .45 pistols. Both went down in a heap on the sidewalk.

Stray bullets hit two people attempting to flee the fire. One died, the contents of his skull scattered behind him in clumps on the asphalt. Gut-shot, a woman writhed in a patch of dirt around a small decorative tree. A man bent to help her as flames leapt over him from the window. Glass peppered them.

A point-blank shotgun blast splattered like raindrops against Bigfoot's left arm and ribcage.

"Mutha fucka!" yelled the bearded shooter. His eyes were wide and intense.

Bigfoot snatched the man's left elbow and tugged, ripping off his arm at the shoulder. Shrieking, the robber fired his shotgun at the sky. A passing seagull jerked in the air and thudded onto a warehouse roof. Blood sprayed from the jagged hole under the man's shoulder.

The robber said, "Mutha *fucka.*" He dropped the shotgun. His backpack slipped off, spilling little vials of clear liquid onto the sidewalk.

Bigfoot smacked him in the side of the head with his ragged arm. As he crumpled, Bigfoot noticed an intricate tattoo of two entwined snakes that writhed from the man's wrist to his bicep—it was Nature Magick. Obviously the man had no idea what the art originally represented, or he would never have ended up with Bigfoot ripping his arm off during a botched robbery attempt.

The big guy with the pistols squirmed out from underneath his dead partner. He ran across the parking lot, firing backwards. He yelled, "No one said any-fucking-thing about fucking Bigfoot!"

Bigfoot roared. He threw the tattooed arm at the zig-zagging gunman, took four long strides and jumped. Somersaulting over the fleeing man, he landed in front of him.

The criminal tried to sidestep Bigfoot. Bigfoot grabbed the man's hands and squeezed, crushing bones against the fat pistol grips and shredding finger flesh. The big man squealed a frantic, high-pitched yelp. Bigfoot squeezed harder and, with one good yank, tore off the guy's arms.

The robber staggered backward, stumbling over the curb

and through some low hedges that bordered the warehouse parking lot. He made strangled gasping sounds and looked crazily at the blood that sprayed from the sides of his chest.

Bigfoot clubbed him with both of his arms, knocking him into a parked VW Beetle. Blood and chunks of muscle splashed all over the car. He tossed the man's arms over his shoulders, picked up the robber by his blood-soaked shirt and chucked him across the lot to where the other criminals lay.

Bigfoot wiped away blood as two uniformed officers pulled into the lot in front of him. They sat under their flashing lights, staring behind him. Bigfoot turned to see what had their attention.

A daycare stood across the street. Tiny faces filled its big picture window—screaming, crying, puking and fainting faces. Daycare workers, also screaming and vomiting, scrambled to move the children away from the window. Bigfoot raised a huge bloody hand and waved daintily. He smiled, which showed off his fangs. The screams intensified.

Bigfoot scooped the arms off the street as he jogged to the stupefied cops in the squad car. He heard the approach of fire trucks and ambulances just as the building across from the parking lot blew up.

Hundreds of gallons of flammable ink stored in plastic drums had ignited a massive explosion. A fireball mixed with ribbons of burning ink and plastic blossomed from the building, pushing cinderblocks, bricks, cars, people and office parts ahead of it. Flaming storage containers flew like fat, erratic missiles in every direction. A cloud of fire erupted with a street-shaking boom.

The windows of the surrounding cars and buildings shattered. Fleeing people pitched to the ground. Sidewalk squares, body parts, flaming car debris, building materials and other flotsam blasted into the air.

Bigfoot ducked behind the squad car while the policemen

inside were splattered with broken glass and burning plastic. He kept the vehicle from skidding and rolling across the lot like others near it, including his own. A spinning chunk of sidewalk tore into the trunk of the squad car and continued through an office building. A cloud of tear gas swirled from the car's trunk, where several canisters had been punctured.

The cops in the car were unconscious and had suffered burns. Bigfoot pulled them out and dragged them around the building to a relatively safe place. Continued explosions dropped scorched bits of concrete and burning plastic siding onto the parking lot and street. A charred cat yowled from a window just above Bigfoot. It jumped onto his back before bounding off into the shadows of the overpass, trailing ashes.

Flaming ink and plastic splashed onto nearby buildings.

Embers scattered across a wide area—some catching in trees and starting them alight. Fire spread. Smaller explosions wracked the building. More bricks and concrete were scattered across the ground. Broken pipes sputtered steam and water. Ashes drifted like thick snow. A flaming tire rolled down the street, straight at the herd of daycare children, who were being ushered downhill to safety. A woman kicked it out of the way.

People from the office building beside the warehouse poured from its exits, coughing due to smoke and tear gas. A woman staggered into Bigfoot and fell on her ass. She prattled, "All my orchids and Henry and the cat and the orchids, oh, the orchids."

Something exploded in the office behind them. A flying pair of scissors speared the woman in the back of her head, severing her brain stem. She said, "Gahhhhhhh."

Propelled by the explosion, several other people cartwheeled into the lot. Glass and sheetrock dropped from the second floor. A large woman in a burning black smock tumbled over the shattered door of a hair salon, a flatiron stuck to her face. She babbled about smoke in her store.

Bigfoot noticed that much of the hair on his arms was singed. He wiped at it and saw naked, sooty skin. He stood up, worrying that his back had probably been scorched, too. He smelled a lot of burnt hair. His shirt was just a collar held together by a loosened necktie, and his pants were gone entirely.

A fire truck barreled through a cloud of black smoke, smoldering cars, an overturned, burning dumpster, most of the wall of the printing company building and a bunch of dazed survivors. Firefighters jumped out and hooked up hoses. Tear gas overtook most of the rescuers quickly, but four managed to put on masks and work to extinguish the closest fire.

Bigfoot tried to help, but he broke the fire hydrant and caused water to spray from the snapped spigot in the wrong direction. Firemen started to yell at him when another explosion launched a volley of burning ink drums. Flames rained down on them.

Bigfoot patted out the fire on one firefighter's back, inadvertently knocking him down and breaking his collarbone and three ribs.

"What the shit?" yelled another fireman. He crouched to help his comrade.

A leg had landed on Bigfoot's shoulder. He flicked it off and decided to let the men deal with the hydrant. Then he secured the backpack and its weird contents.

Flame retardant and water hissed against burning buildings. A helicopter hovered overhead. Distant crashes sounded from the freeway as some people slowed to see what was happening below them while others did not. Traffic clogged the 405 Bridge.

An electrical pole fell into the daycare. Thick, snaking wires whipped around the puddled street. Three firefighters and a man who hopped on his remaining leg were knocked down and electrocuted. Sparks erupted from electrical boxes and ignited two other fires. Flames crawled up the wall of a gym, causing people in spandex to run out into the street, adding to the mayhem.

Roiling smoke choked the air. People moaned and cried. A few gurgled and whimpered. Others cursed Bigfoot as they stumbled past or dragged themselves toward an arriving ambulance.

A hundred cops converged on the scene. Guns drawn, they picked their way to the epicenter of the chaos.

Bigfoot handed the backpack to his lieutenant, who told him that he'd better get his ass over to the chief's office. He even said, "Pronto." The douche.

The chief was bright red. He paced behind his desk, holding a golf trophy in his pudgy hand, and it looked like he was going to throw it. Sweat soaked his light blue work shirt under his arms and down his round sides. His tie was too tight, as usual. It seemed like his bald tomato head was going to pop. "Goddamnit, Bigfoot! How many goddamn times do I have to tell you that you can't go around pulling off people's arms, smashing goddamn cars, killing suspects—and goddamn civilians—and wrecking every goddamn thing in sight? You blew up a goddamn city block! I can't keep making it okay with the mayor and the city council and the goddamn media. This is the last goddamn straw."

Bigfoot knew that the chief was trying to quit smoking, and it was difficult for him. He was also addicted to caffeine and suffered from acid indigestion. He was at least seventy pounds overweight. Bigfoot didn't meet the chief's bugged-out eyes. He picked at the singed hair on his leg, worrying that the fat little man would have a heart attack and he'd lose the last connection he had with his adopted father, who'd been the chief's best friend and partner.

"I'm transferring you to Missing Persons. They need some help over there. Got a bunch of missing people."

Bigfoot's jaw dropped. Slowly closing his mouth, he growled at the chief.

"I'm partnering you with Lyle Straits. He retires in five months, and at that time your performance will be evaluated. The goddamn Missing Persons Unit is safe, boring, and should not involve pulling anyone's goddamn arms off. Got it? Stay off the goddamn news."

Bigfoot fidgeted on the floor. He couldn't really sit in chairs, and sitting on the floor put him closer to eye-level and made it easier to work with computers, eat in restaurants or at people's houses and whatever else required being at table or desk level.

The chief stopped pacing and lowered his voice. He said, "Straits isn't real happy with this, either. He's about as big a loner as you. But he's a goddamn good cop. Take it easy on the old guy. I told Lieutenant Jacobi at MPU to let you two pretty much do your own thing—figured you would, anyway. So just get along and find missing people or some shit. You know our relationship won't mean dick if you keep going goddamn crazy. Now get out of my goddamn office!" He slammed the trophy on his desk.

Chapter 2

Bigfoot drove his monster truck to his massive cabin just outside a small town called Gales Creek, about thirty-five miles west of Portland. He'd built the cabin himself. It covered nearly an acre of the ten he owned. Most everything inside was Bigfoot-sized.

He considered running over the paparazzi. They gathered around their cars alongside the road. None had dared venture up the drive since "the driveway incident" five years ago.

Inside the cabin, Bigfoot poured three cans of root beer into a giant stein, started a fire and peeked out a living room window. He was glad to see that most of the paparazzi were gone.

He took a seat on the couch and looked at the photos displayed on the mantle—those of his wife, Lara, and adoptive father. He thought about the chief and what he'd said.

The chief was like an uncle to him, and one of the few reasons he didn't give up on humanity. After losing his wife and unborn child, Bigfoot often wondered if he should leave the civilized world and fade into the wilderness for good.

He'd met Lara soon after he'd been promoted to detective. His wit, sense of humor and gentle strength had hooked her. Plus, she loved him. Genuinely.

Prior to this, Bigfoot had given up on anyone

understanding him, wanting to grow with him and be his most intimate friend. And then there she was at Saturday Market, selling the most tasty heritage tomatoes in all of the Pacific Northwest. She laughed when he ate a whole tomato as a sample, and her voice was like a sunny waterfall to all of his senses. By writing on her pricing chalkboard, he asked her if she liked climbing trees. Beside the question, he drew a funny cartoon of himself hanging from a tree. This made her laugh more. She went hiking with him the next day.

Lara got pregnant a year after they were married. Their marriage wasn't perfect—no marriage was—but there was still much joy in it. He couldn't imagine himself with another woman. She was his soul mate.

Then the Sasquatch Hunter, a crazed murderer who'd targeted Bigfoot, slaughtered her and the child in her womb.

Bigfoot drained the last of the root beer. *Missing Persons. What bullshit.*

He went outside, howled from the porch and threw rocks into the forest. While he hung upside-down from his favorite pine tree, being grumpy, Syd showed up. The kid and his mom were Bigfoot's closest neighbors.

Syd said, "I heard you screaming and chucking stuff."

Bigfoot climbed down from the tree and sat on the porch. Syd sat beside him.

"You okay?" Syd asked.

"Baaaaaaaad day," he said.

"Yeah, I saw it on the news."

Bigfoot liked Syd because he understood nature and never talked to him like he was an animal, rock-star, or monster. Since Syd's mom was deaf, the kid knew sign language. This made Syd one of the few people with whom Bigfoot could have conversations in complete sentences. Sometimes he wished he'd find an adult friend who could sign like Lara, who'd learned in order to better communicate with him. But the kid was smart, funny, and wise for his age.

Bigfoot trusted Syd. He was one of a select group who knew Bigfoot's real name: Whistler.

It was his people's belief that to reveal one's name too often lessened one's Magick. Most everyone always called him "Bigfoot," anyway. It bothered him at first, but he grew to appreciate the generalization. It reminded him to always protect the secrets of his people, though he knew only a scant few of them: how to be nearly invisible among trees or ride the wind; how to speak with animals and sometimes see through their eyes. He knew to keep his name sacred.

Syd asked, "Wanna whittle?"

Bigfoot smiled. He reached over and dragged between them the box with their latest work and tools.

Syd retrieved the *idol* he was carving: a naked woman with a chainsaw arm.

"Her boobs are too big," Bigfoot signed.

"Boobs can never be too big," Syd replied.

Bigfoot laughed and shook his head. He pulled his carving from the box as Syd resumed work.

Whittling was something he and the boy liked to do together. Bigfoot used a Bowie knife to carve fantastically realistic animals from hardwood. Syd was pretty good, for a twelve-year-old, but he liked to talk more than work.

They sat for a couple of hours and chatted about wilderness survival. Bigfoot taught Syd a new birdcall and the names of several plants he'd not yet learned. The kid left with a promise to return the next day.

Bigfoot watched Syd walk down the road, realizing that he loved him. He considered the fragility of humans and their steely strengths: babies born without the ability to walk or survive without their protective parents; humanity's consuming, lying, believing, obeying, rebelling, defeating, and assuming. The negative aspects of society were piling upon the chief every day, killing him. Bigfoot loved the chief, too. He thought he could wade through the bullshit a little longer, if only for people like him and Syd.

Bigfoot made sage and horsetail tea, lounged on his extra-long couch and listened to a few songs from INXS, which made him think about Australia. He closed his eyes and imagined flocks of parrots and cockatoos whirling through a forest of gum trees. He wondered how those forests smelled and if Yowies, the hairy wild-men of the bush, were real.

Bigfoot finished his tea and went to sleep in his giant hammock. He dreamt he was five-years-old again, and Detective Cassidy Oldman was rescuing him from the poachers who had just killed his mother.

Cassidy held out his hand. He said, "Come here, little guy. I'll help you."

Whistler wasn't that little, comparatively. He looked at the man and tried to gauge his motivations. Whistler had a natural wariness about humankind. He knew to be invisible to them. But he could see kindness and care reflected in the detective's eyes.

He heard the approach of those who'd killed his mother. Whistler was conflicted. He knew he could most likely stay alive by himself, but, apart from his mother, he hadn't seen another of his kind in a year. He didn't want to be alone.

Branches snapped. A poacher hissed, "I think there's another of 'em."

Whistler whispered the *dead words* in his mother's ear, and her body began to fade. He ran to the man and took his hand. As they retreated into the dark of the forest, Whistler looked back to what remained of his mother's body—a pile of hair, already blowing away—and signed goodbyes.

Chapter 3

The next morning, Bigfoot met his new partner, Lyle, for breakfast. Bigfoot arrived first. He ordered a dozen donuts and three large coffees. Pushing a chair away from a table, he sat on the floor. Donut shop floors weren't so bad, but he rarely sat on them in bars or fast food joints.

Lyle arrived twenty minutes late. He sneezed on Bigfoot's remaining donuts, which Bigfoot then couldn't eat. Lyle looked the part of an older TV detective—overweight, mostly in the belly, balding, constantly sweating, and eye rolling like someone who'd long since stopped giving a fuck about his job or much of anything else. His badly tied, bland necktie, complete with coffee stains, spoke volumes.

Lyle said, "I'm allergic to all animal dander. Hmm. I thought you'd smell bad."

Bigfoot didn't bother to explain that he took showers, or that Lyle *was* an animal. He drank from the mug that resembled a doll's teacup in his huge hand.

Lyle said, "We'll be desk jockeys in the MPU, which is fine with me. I'm about to retire. I'm old, fat, and done with this bullshit. I just want to fly-fish and eat my wife's cooking until I die peacefully in my sleep after my daughter marries a doctor and has two cute little kids who'll call me *Grampy* and bring me my cane whenever I leave my fishin' chair."

Bigfoot shook his head. He had other ideas about

missing person cases, like following leads and finding the people. He opened the notebook he used to communicate. Adorning the cover was a collage of chainsaw-wielding bears and eagles, attacking men against a mountainous backdrop. He uncapped a fine-tipped Sharpie and wrote inside: I hate sitting at a desk.

Lyle sneezed. "It's better than a stakeout, or draggin' dead bodies out of the river. I'm tellin' you, I'm all for riding a desk these last few months. Look, I know all about your hotshot career. Youngest detective in city history, nearly single-handedly solving capers like the Kombucha Heist, Sugar-Coated Sophie's street-performer sex-slave operation, the River Water Scandal, the Portlandia kidnapping/mass-shooting, the Bomb Dog, and the dismantling of the Diablo Quinoa Cartel. You also lost two partners in the line of duty and have been a lone wolf since the last one, four years ago. Not that I don't have lists like that of my own. In my day… Anyhow, I'm sayin' this is a good gig. And we're gonna take it easy."

Bigfoot said, "Psshhh."

Lieutenant Jacobi welcomed them to the squad, showed them around and introduced everyone.

He said, "We run a tight ship here." From his cadence, his high-and-tight haircut and the immaculate tuck of his shirt in his slacks, Bigfoot knew he'd been a Marine.

Before Jacobi left, he told Bigfoot and Lyle to just jump right in and see what they could learn. This suited each of them fine.

The other cops in the unit weren't very friendly to Bigfoot. Only one female officer named Anna paid him any attention. She came to his desk to make sure he was settling in okay.

She told him, "There have been more people reported missing from the area in the past six months than in the previous six years combined. Everyone in the MPU is scrambling to find answers. It doesn't seem random."

Any leads? Bigfoot wrote in his notebook.

"Not anything, really. Two missing people from the past four months were recovered, one a suicide and the other a runaway husband in Vegas. Otherwise, we've been stumped."

Is there a comprehensive list of missing people?

"I'll email it to you." Anna smiled. "It's kinda cool to be working with you."

Bigfoot returned the smile. He wrote down his email address and tore the paper out of his notebook.

Anna took it back to her desk.

Bigfoot watched her walk away. He was glad that someone in the department had been sweet, helpful and kind to him. That rarely occurred in new situations.

While Lyle pretended to examine files, Bigfoot created lists and organized strategies. He set up several interviews with friends and families of local people who'd gone missing in the past year. He drank a lot of coffee, straight from the pot on his desk.

Lyle wasn't happy about the interviews, which started the next day. He sneezed the whole time he read the memo Bigfoot had written to explain his plan to pursue the cases. He said, "I don't know what meeting the families is gonna do."

Bigfoot wrote: I just want to see if any patterns emerge.

Lyle grumbled about the first meeting being at eight in the morning. "Won't even have time to shave. Can't ever get in the fuckin' bathroom. Teenage girls..."

Bigfoot went home early and whittled with Syd, who had been waiting for him on the porch. He let the boy spend as much time in and around his cabin as he wanted, just as long as he stayed away from his root beer and weed. Bigfoot knew that Syd's home life was often difficult.

Syd's mom, Vikki, had a different boyfriend nearly every month. And all of them were the same type: big, hairy, drunk, chauvinistic, stupid and mean. He was sure not a single one knew how to sign. But they weren't with her to talk. Vikki worked as a dancer at a club downtown. She found her boyfriends there. It wasn't the best place to shop for love.

Vikki had tried to seduce Bigfoot a few times, and though he found her very attractive, she'd been drunk every instance and he'd declined her advances. Bigfoot rarely saw her sober. It was the only reason he hadn't asked Vikki over for dinner in the year since she and Syd had moved into the trailer half a mile down the road.

Bigfoot asked Syd, "Do you want to learn how to talk like a squirrel?"

"Hell yes!"

He chattered some squirrel talk—just a simple, "Hello, I hope your day is treeful."

Chapter 4

Bigfoot and Lyle interviewed three families of missing people in the morning.

Mrs. Decker made four pots of coffee while she showed them seven photo albums. Her seventeen-year-old daughter Kelsey had been missing for three months. She also had been in girl scouts, played in parks, took family trips to Yellowstone and Canada, went to countless school dances, was in the audience of a concert, did a few photo-shoots, had been in a hot air balloon, went camping a million times, roller-bladed, dated a few boys, drove cars, and decorated cakes.

After viewing sixty photos of said confections, Mrs. Decker asked, "Would you like some cake?"

Lyle said yes. Bigfoot declined.

Kelsey's mother hadn't embraced the digital age of photography until recently. "Would you officers like to see my photo files on the computer? I only have about three years of them."

Lyle spoke with a mouthful of cake, "We're detectives, ma'am. And no, thank you. We've seen all we need." He handed her his card, finished the last bite of goopy chocolate and assured her that they would find her daughter.

Bigfoot drove them to Northeast Portland. Lyle started sneezing as soon as he got in the car. He complained about being smooshed against the door. Crunched up against the steering wheel, Bigfoot shrugged as best he could. He knocked Lyle with his elbow when he turned left.

The Hugos, parents of an eight-year-old who went missing in the middle of the night, had differing opinions about what had happened to their son.

After explaining the circumstances of his disappearance, commenting on Bigfoot smelling nice and showing them her son's room, Janice Hugo said, "Someone took him. I just want him back."

Her husband Rob said, "I think the little punk ran away and joined the circus."

Janice shook her head and sighed.

Lyle asked, "Is there a reason you'd think that? Has Brendan ever said he wanted to join the circus?"

Rob put his fried egg sandwich on the TV tray beside him. He glanced over from the show he was watching to scowl at Lyle. "No. Jus' seems like something the little turd would do."

Bigfoot growled.

Janice said, "Rob isn't Brendan's real dad."

"So fuckin' what?" Rob asked through a dribbly bite of his sandwich.

Lyle stood. "Okay. Well, I think we have all we need from you at this point. Here's my card. You can call if you think of anything else that might be important. We'll do what we can to find your son."

Bigfoot hunched over Rob.

Rob looked up from the TV. "Check the circus," he said.

Bigfoot showed his teeth.

Lyle hustled him out the door. He knew that Bigfoot was jittery from all the coffee. "I'll drive," he said. When he opened the driver side door of the sedan and saw the squashed seat covered in hair, he sneezed. "You drive."

Both Bigfoot and Lyle could tell they were in for a strange experience when they entered the next house, ushered inside by a large, teenaged girl who wore a too-tight t-shirt with Bigfoot's face stretched over her breasts. She didn't say a word, but smiled and bobbed her head up and down. The door opened to a room overflowing with Bigfoot-related items.

Lyle sneezed.

Bigfoot stood hunched over, staring at the décor.

The girl closed the door and yelled, "Ma! MA! BIGFOOT is here! BIGFOOT COP IS IN OUR HOUSE!" She squealed, scrunched her face up and bounced on her heels. She stood there jiggling while the detectives looked around the room.

Posters covered nearly every wall. Bigfoot at the police academy—a close up of him wearing a tiny gray sweatshirt at the firing range. Bigfoot with his Rangers team. Bigfoot fighting a great white shark (he hadn't really done that—it was some Internet meme). Bigfoot flipping a car. Bigfoot in his monster truck, driving over a car during an off-duty bank robbery pursuit. Bigfoot giving a big thumbs-up while judging a bikini contest. Countless smaller photos of Bigfoot, newspaper clippings and magazine covers filled the gaps between posters.

Every surface in the room was plastered with Bigfoot stuff.

There were figurines, footprint casts, fan club certificates, books on Bigfoot, stuffed dolls of various sizes, boxes with Bigfoot carved on them or with his photo lacquered to their tops, Bigfoot root beer bottles, Bigfoot action figures and Lego sets, mugs with Bigfoot's face or sayings on them like, *#1 Bigfoot Lover* and *I Saw Bigfoot!*, a life-sized Bigfoot bust, a model of his monster truck, two Bigfoot clocks, stacks of postcards, and at least a dozen bottles of *Duke Agro's Bigfoot-Scented Room Atmosphere Spray* scattered on tables, dressers and the fireplace mantle.

A nearly life-sized blow-up Bigfoot doll loomed in one corner of the room. In another, a hairy Bigfoot arm on a thick wooden base held a floor lamp like an Olympic torch. The lampshade was adorned with Bigfoot silhouettes.

A flash from the stairs shook the detectives out of their trance.

"Oh my God! Bigfoot is in my *house*!" A woman almost as thick as Bigfoot wobbled down the stairs wearing Bigfoot slippers and a jogging suit with Bigfoot's head emblazoned on the breast. She snapped another photo of the bewildered Bigfoot and sneezing Lyle.

The flash blinded Bigfoot. He tripped backward over the coffee table, crushing it and knocking off the bust, which bounced on the thick shag carpet. He fell into the overstuffed leather couch with a crunch.

The woman took another photo as he fell, pushing Lyle out of her way to get different angles of the shot. She said, "Oh. My. God. Bigfoot is wrecking my house! Get this on video, Claire!"

The girl, still bouncing up and down, pulled out her phone to capture the moment.

Bigfoot roared.

Lyle waved his hands and sneezed. "Everyone calm down!"

A gangly teenaged boy came into the room from the hall. He was eating an apple. "Crap, Mom, give the guy some room." He waved at Bigfoot. "Hey."

Bigfoot untangled himself from the mangled couch. He knocked over a side table, upsetting a Bigfoot poker set, scattering Bigfoot-faced poker chips and Bigfoot cards.

The boy said, "Let's go out back." He led them to the backyard.

His mother and sister stayed inside. They peered out the kitchen window and took photos.

Lyle said, "What in the shit is going on in there?"

The kid flipped his red hair out of his face and said, "My mom and sister are a bit obsessed." He extended his hand to Bigfoot. "I'm Nate Winters. My twin brother Kyle is the missing one. He walked to the store on the corner, but he didn't come home. We filed a report and stuff."

Bigfoot shook his hand and then wrote in his notebook: We've read the report. We're just following up. He showed it to Nate.

Nate threw the apple core over the fence. "Right. Well... I talked to the clerk. He knows us. He said he sold Kyle a blue raspberry soda, a pack of Big League Chew and a lighter. No one strange had been in before. Nothing was weird at all. I'm sure that's in the report."

Lyle said, "Yeah, it is. We're just new on the case. We want to get a good perspective on your brother's home life."

Nate shrugged. "Kyle didn't run away. Sometimes we both want to—with all the... Bigfoot stuff. I mean, we eat Bigfoot frozen vegetables, Bigfoot waffles, Bigfoot cereal. Bigfoot root beer is pretty good. And up until we turned sixteen last year, they dragged us to Bigfoot Con, BF Con *and* BigCon, Bigfoot Lovers Gatherings, Bigfoot the Game Tournaments and The International Bigfoot LARP Festival. No offense, but it's a bit much to take."

Bigfoot wrote in his notebook: I can't take another minute of it.

Lyle said, "Thanks, Nate. We'll be in touch if we learn anything new." He handed the kid his card. "Tell your mom the city will replace the couch and table. Have her call the police station and tell them what happened."

Bigfoot wrote: Can we leave through the yard?

Nate smiled. "Yeah, there's a gate on the side of the house."

Bigfoot peeled out as Nate's mother and sister tumbled out the front door, shouting and snapping photos.

The detectives decided to go downtown for lunch.

They sat in the park near the food carts. Bigfoot was popping falafel balls into his mouth, five at a time, when Lyle asked him why he didn't eat meat.

Bigfoot scribbled in his notebook: I talk to animals. Don't want to eat them.

"Hmm," Lyle said. He bit into his bacon cheeseburger. Then he sneezed bits of chewed meat and bun onto his shoes.

Bigfoot noticed an overdressed man in a tailored suit sitting across from them in the park, reading a *Portland Monthly* magazine and pretending to pay no attention to the detectives. He smelled like expensive cologne and cigarettes, though he wasn't smoking. A group of street kids wandered between them and when they straggled past, bumming money from business people on their lunch breaks, he was gone.

When the detectives were getting into their car, a group of young women shouted from across the street at them. The women ran over with their phones out, asking Bigfoot if they could take photos with him, crowding Lyle out of the way and eventually making him take photos using all their phones. Bigfoot posed for several shots with the girls. He tried to remember to hold his head up straight. He looked like an idiot when he let it fall to the side, which was easy to do when posing with tiny humans.

After the women scurried away, giggling and waving, Lyle said, "Does that sort of thing happen a lot?"

Bigfoot shrugged and got into the car.

Lyle watched the girls compare photos as they walked down the street.

A goateed, clipboard-holding man with slicked-back hair greeted Lyle as he reached for the door. "Hello, sir. How's *your* day going?"

"What? Oh. I have indigestion, and I've spent the morning talking to weirdos like you."

The man smiled wider. "That's great! My day's been fantastic, thank you. So, I'm wondering if you've heard about the Democratic Organization for Rounded Corners of Safety?"

Lyle tried to squeeze past the guy. He said, "Not interested."

The guy moved more into Lyle's way. "Well, it is unfortunate that you don't care about the well-being of all the children in America."

"I didn't say that. Move along."

"I'm sorry, but I'm enjoying my rights as a citizen of this failing country." The man spoke louder and louder. "I am allowed to stand on the public sidewalk and speak my mind freely. Even to bullies like you. It's violent bullies like you that made the states look like guns to begin with. It's citizens like me who fight within our rights to change abusive things like that. Change the map; change the world."

Lyle stopped trying to push his way around the guy. "What?"

"Just sign this petition to get the corners rounded off on all the states that look like guns and I'll stop talking to you."

Lyle looked the man up and down. "Move."

The guy shouted, "California! Delaware! Florida! Idaho! Illinois, Kentucky, Louisiana, New Hampshire, New Jersey, New York, North Carolina, Oklahoma, Tennessee,

Texas, Vermont and Virginia! Make them round! Make them round! Make them round!" He pumped his fist in the air.

Lyle's gun-hand twitched.

Bigfoot got out of the car.

The man jumped backward. "Oh! Oh! Bigfoot! The most violent of them all!" He looked at Lyle and realized he was a cop. "Pigs! Pigs!" He skipped backward, holding his clipboard in front of him like a shield, and ran away shouting, "Change the map; change the world! Change the map; change the world!"

Lyle said, "Texas doesn't look like a gun."

Bigfoot shrugged. He thought Tennessee was a bit of a stretch, too.

After lunch, they managed to interview two other families about their missing children.

Oswaldo Marachinato was a sad man who slouched on a battered couch in a dusty room and wailed about his missing nine-year-old daughter, Marianna. He wrung a faded handkerchief in his papery hands. His daughter had been missing for three days.

Missing posters were strewn across the coffee table. One was tacked to the threshold leading to the kitchen.

"She's a good girl. Yes, maybe sometimes she steal. And she do that thing with push her grandma down the stairs. And there was the time where she bake those live rats in the Christmas turkey. I mean, except for few things like gathering fingernails from schoolmates, the burnings, Spider Day, living taxidermy, her mama and the scissors, the thing I read in her diary about how she stalk Amanda Bynes and make her crazy, her bear semen collection, the basement, that stuff she say about hitting my temples with hammer if I don't buy her new phone... Other than those little things, she's such a sweetie. Why would anyone take my Marianna?" Oswaldo sobbed into his handkerchief.

Bigfoot stared at the man.

Lyle said, "Uh. Hm. Um. Well. What makes you think someone took her?"

"She love her mama and papa. She wouldn't leave us on purpose." He sobbed some more.

Lyle looked at Bigfoot. He said, "Um, Mr. Marachinato, can we, um, see Marianna's room?"

Bigfoot shook his head.

Lyle kicked his hairy butt. He mouthed, "Get *up*."

Oswaldo pointed down the hall.

Reluctantly, Bigfoot followed Lyle to the girl's room. A blood-red handprint was painted on the door, and the words, *FUCK OFF AND DIE* were carved into the wood. Bigfoot didn't think he wanted to find *this* missing person.

He was sure of it when they opened the door.

The room was black, floor to ceiling. Even the window glass was blacked out. Paintings of headless animals and enlarged autopsy photographs added color to the walls. A portrait of Marianna in a black Victorian dress, holding a mutilated doll with blood trickling out of the corner of its smirking mouth, hung alone on the far wall. A smoky quartz crystal ball sat in the middle of the floor on an altar made of dog and cat bones. Bigfoot could smell them—four dogs and six cats went into its construction.

There was a kind of crude, dirty lab set up in the corner near the black-bedecked four-poster bed. Cages stacked atop aquariums took up the wall near the lab—bugged-out rats, lethargic lizards, hamsters lying on their backs, a shivering dog, two snakes, some hairless mice, a patchy squirrel, a marmot with two tails, and a raccoon whose mask had been plucked all started to scream at Bigfoot.

"Let us out!"

"Thank Gaia, Bigfoot's here!"

"Don't let the snakes near us!"

"This girl is sick! She sewed my friend Maggie to a fucking lizard!"

"Hey, that fucking lizard was my husband!"

"Let us out!"

The fish darted around making fish noises, but Bigfoot couldn't understand them. A turtle stuck his head out of one of the tanks and started to explain the situation carefully.

Bigfoot cut them all off with a raspy growl. He picked up the crystal ball and heaved it through the window.

Lyle sneezed and backed out of the room.

A woman shouted from the room next door. "What the fuck you doin' now, Oswaldo, you shrivel-dick come-spatter? Warm up some fucking meatloaf for me, Bitch! I'm watchin' the *X-Files* marathon again and this is a good episode—the one where the secret agents are dressed like aliens and they get abducted by that demon Bigfoot lookin' *real* alien and get all anal probed and shit. Like should happen to *you*! And if you broke another mirror, so help me the fuck god I will rip you a new asshole and fuck you in it with my bloated titty, you scrotum-sucking chicken fucker. Meatloaf! Now!"

Sneezing, Lyle ran out of the house.

Oswaldo ignored his wife and moaned about his darling Marianna.

Bigfoot ferried the animals out the window. He made sure to let the snakes out last.

He carried the six aquariums past the grieving Oswaldo and out the front door. He loaded them into the backseat of the sedan. The turtle started a long-winded protest, but Bigfoot tuned him out.

Lyle sneezed the whole way to the river, where Bigfoot freed the fish and turtle. He hoped it wouldn't kill them.

At their next stop, a wrinkled lady with her hair tied into

a tight bun pointed a shotgun at them. A cigarette dangled between her raisin lips. She had filed a report five months prior stating that Bigfoot had abducted her son. She said that Bigfoot had come down in a flying saucer and shot a blue beam at her son to knock him out before taking him to space. She also said that her son was conceived immaculately.

She said, "I've been protecting him from Reptilians and the Illuminati, but I hadn't even *thought* about alien Bigfoot snatching him up while I was out back photographing chemtrails."

Just getting her to allow Bigfoot to wait outside the door on the front porch so he could hear her was a chore. He didn't listen long, anyway. He went to the backyard with the cat that lived there to talk about what had happened to the kid.

The cat said, "He stole what he could and took off. I heard him talking to someone on the phone about Washington since it was legal to smoke pot there. I don't care, really. Don't pay much attention to those fucking whackjobs. Lady feeds me well and mostly leaves me alone, so I'm fine."

Lyle met Bigfoot in the car forty-five minutes later. "Runaway."

Bigfoot nodded and started the car.

They went to the station to file reports and consider what they'd learned, if anything. Bigfoot doubted that the interviews had done much good thus far.

Ten minutes after they arrived, Lyle said, "It's five. I have to go. My wife will kill me if I'm not there for Thursday dinner. Thursday dinner is a big deal. It's Taco Night. The whole family has to be at the table by exactly six-fifteen—dressed up, clean fingernails, smiles—or she flips out and won't cook for a week. It really sucks when that happens. You have no idea."

Bigfoot stayed late and gathered the evidence into categories, sticking pushpins in a map of the city and surrounding area, hanging up photos on the corkboard, separating them into age groups and generally arranging things to better continue the investigation. He had several more meetings scheduled over the next few weeks.

He looked at the photos on the wall. Sixty-five people reported missing in the Portland area in the previous six months. That seemed extreme to Bigfoot. Forty-seven were children. That bothered him. Except for that Marianna chick—it was fine that she was gone. Bigfoot shuddered. He didn't look forward to the other meetings he had scheduled, but he hoped to find a pattern, or, at the very least, some sort of lead.

Chapter 5

The next day Bigfoot and Lyle went to Lincoln High School. Peyton Miller had left volleyball practice on her bike the week before and headed home. Her bike was found the next day, four blocks from her house, but there was no other trace of Peyton.

Bigfoot wanted to start by speaking to the volleyball coach and maybe some of Peyton's friends. He parked in front of the Westside Grocery.

The detectives crossed the street to the school and checked in at the office.

The woman at the desk jumped when Bigfoot ducked through the doorway. She yelled, "Holy *Christ*! I thought you were a bear! You should wear an orange cap or something."

Lyle laughed.

A bear? Bigfoot scowled and stepped back into the hall, letting his partner deal with the woman. Unfortunately, it wasn't the first time someone had suggested he wear hunter's orange clothing.

Bigfoot walked slowly along the hall while he waited for Lyle. He liked going into places like libraries, hospitals and schools because he could stand up straight inside. The station had low ceilings, though it was connected to City Hall, which was full of wide-open space. Bigfoot liked the gym, too.

In the gym, the coach told them, "Peyton's a good

student, excellent athlete, nice person, has great hair, her teeth are perfect, her volleyball shorts fit her better than any other girl's fit, and she's got this cute little pout when I tell her she has to stay after class. Oh, man, her nipples are like pointy drops of rosebud latex, especially in my air-conditioned office during extra-credit calisthenics."

Bigfoot glared at the woman.

The coach cleared her throat and watched the girls doing jumping jacks in front of them, as she'd instructed.

Lyle asked, "Does Peyton have any enemies?"

She frowned. "I don't think so. I mean, she's so popular and beautiful and bouncy and gorgeous and sweet and smells like a musky flower dipped in honey. Maybe the ugly girls."

Peyton's friends said the same sorts of things about Peyton being popular and gorgeous, but a couple of them added that she was a skinny bitch whose daddy bought her everything and she rubbed it in everyone's faces and who the hell did she think she was, anyway?

A few of them seemed genuinely upset that she was missing, and all of them were afraid something terrible had happened to her, like she'd been raped and murdered by someone with the Elephant Man disease, or had amnesia and was somewhere in Europe, scribbling weird tattoos on herself and giving backpackers blowjobs at icky foreign hostels, or was a trucker's slave, kept captive in the bed-part of their big, gross trucker trucks, high on crystal meth, turning tricks at truck-stops for scraps of bacon. They were afraid that it would happen to them next. Six of Peyton's friends had made a pact to remain in constant text, Skype, or even physical contact so that they would not meet the same fate.

Lyle suggested they see if there were any good muffins at the convenience store as the detectives walked back to the car.

An ogre-like man with a pockmarked face exited the store carrying a six-pack of beer. A Vietnamese guy, about the size of a twelve-year-old girl, ran behind him, yelling, "Hey! Stop! He no pay! He no pay! Help! Help!"

The shoplifter looked over his shoulder and waved his hand dismissively at the pursuing storeowner.

When he turned around, Bigfoot faced him.

Bigfoot grabbed the man's six-pack-gripping-hand and tugged. The man screeched as his arm was torn from its socket. He fell to the sidewalk, kicking and screaming. A fountain of blood sprayed parked cars and pooled in the gutter.

Lyle said, "Oh, fuck." He tried, simultaneously, to stop the bleeding with a discarded paper bag and pull out his phone to call the station.

Bigfoot pried the beer out of the man's jerking fingers, splashing Lyle and the shopkeeper with blood. The shoplifter turned gray. Bigfoot handed the beer to the shop owner. The little man clutched the six-pack to his chest and backed into his store.

Two men smoking cigarettes stood on the porch above the store. One yelled down, "Good job, Bigfoot! That asshole's been stealing from them for a month."

The other said, "Wooo!" and took a photo with his phone.

Bigfoot dropped the man's arm and waved. He thought, *Uh oh.*

Lyle, coated in blood, looked up at him. "Jesus, Bigfoot! You can't just— What the fuck?"

An ambulance arrived, and the EMTs said the guy was dead.

Bigfoot stood hunched over in the chief's office with his head down. He saw Lyle leaning against the coffee station outside.

"I just can't believe that on a goddamn missing persons interview, you managed to rip someone's goddamn arms off," the chief said. He wasn't yelling. He *was* smoking. *Inside.*

Bigfoot held up one finger.

The chief raised his voice. "Don't get smart, Bigfoot. *One* goddam arm. It doesn't matter." He ashed his cigarette on the floor.

Bigfoot stared at his toes.

"The point is, I put you in MPU so that you wouldn't cause a scene and kill a goddamn shoplifter at nine o'clock in the morning on a goddamn downtown sidewalk! *Not* do that. You goddamn specifically goddamn told me that you goddamn wouldn't, goddamn it!" The chief was red again. He crushed his cigarette in his mini Zen garden.

Bigfoot started writing in his notebook.

The chief yelled, "I don't give a goddamn goddamn what you have to say! This is it, Bigfoot! One more fuck up and you are in serious goddamn trouble! I had better not hear a word about you on TV, in the paper, online, or anywhere outside of your goddamn lieutenant telling me what a good, quiet goddamn job you are doing at being good and quiet! Now get out of my goddamn office!"

Bigfoot slunk out, closing the door behind him.

The chief shouted through the glass, "Last goddamn straw!"

Lyle asked, "How many last straws have you had?"

Bigfoot smiled and flashed ten fingers again and again and again and again.

The rest of the week went the same—the detectives interviewing friends, family and co-workers about missing people.

Bigfoot got to better know his partner. He learned that, at Lyle's house, Monday was Fried Chicken and Football Night. Tuesday was Middle Eastern Buffet. Wednesday was Pizza Night. Thursday was the infamous Taco Night where everyone had to be on time or his wife freaked out. On Fridays, Lyle liked to skip out of work around lunchtime, if he could, for fishing trips or camping at the coast. He barbequed on the weekends, at home or away, rain or shine.

Bigfoot chopped vegetables on his black shale kitchen counter. He heard a high-pitched whine. He checked his iPod, but it wasn't turned on. He didn't have a TV. His laptop was on, but it wasn't making the sound. Neither was his phone. He found the source of the sound after one pass through the living room. It was a potted fern.

More accurately, it was the tiny, malfunctioning wireless camera hidden among the plant's fronds.

He pulled it out of the plant, snarled into its lens and popped it between his fingers.

Then he emailed his acquaintance in the electronics division and asked to have a squad come to sweep his house.

Bigfoot went from room to room while he waited for them, searching corners, sculptures and vents. He discovered a few more cameras and two microphones.

It wasn't the first time he'd been bugged. But it had been awhile. And it made him wonder who was watching him.

The electronics guys found eleven more cameras and twenty-three listening devices in and around his cabin. They left with the assurance that they would track down whoever had put them there.

Bigfoot doubted they would. He figured it was likely the government. People in power tended to be suspicious of him, no matter what agreements he'd signed. He knew that several agencies surveilled him.

He returned to making dinner.

His phone vibrated on the kitchen table. A text. He ignored it until he'd sat down to eat. And then his appetite was ruined. It read: I CAN STILL SEE YOU.

Bigfoot looked around the room. Surely, those guys had done a good job cleaning the place. He peered at his reflection in the window. *Someone outside*, he thought. He stomped out the kitchen door to the backyard.

Trees whispered in the slight wind as rain fell. Bigfoot peered into the shadows.

He called the number that had texted him.

He heard a phone ring in the distant forest. He charged after the sound.

It was a disposable phone, wedged in the branches of a pine tree. Shoeprints covered the muddy ground below the tree. Someone had paced back and forth. Bigfoot looked toward his lighted kitchen window. They'd been watching him for a while.

He followed the tracks away from the cabin. They led uphill and then back down. By the time Bigfoot realized that whoever had left them had doubled back, he heard a truck engine. He bolted through the forest, but only caught the glow of taillights as the truck sped onto the highway at the end of the road.

"Raaaaaaaaaawwwwwwwwwwwwrrrrrrrrrrrrrr!" Bigfoot yelled.

The next day, after dropping off the phone to be fingerprinted and perhaps tracked to the seller, Bigfoot ate cold veggie lasagna and drank root beer for lunch behind the police station. He was there to meet with a murder of crows. He was disappointed in his investigation. Thus far there were no clear patterns. A few of the missing people had obviously run away. The ones that seemed to have been abducted didn't fit any specific group, though. Their ages varied, just like their backgrounds. Nearly half were males and half females. Bigfoot decided it was time to get help.

He showed the crows photos of the missing people on his laptop, which was a *bitch* for him to use, and asked them to keep an eye out. Only one person was familiar to the crows—a man with a red mohawk named Clive who'd fed them. They expressed how sorry they were that he was missing, several of them saying that they'd wondered where he'd gone, and promised to watch for everyone on Bigfoot's list.

One crow remarked on how many of the missing people had red hair. He said, "I really like red-haired people because their hair glows in ultraviolet."

Bigfoot thought about what the crow had said. He realized that out of the sixty-five people, forty-three had red hair. This did not seem like a coincidence. It seemed like a lead. Finally.

He thanked the crows.

"No worries!"

"Happy to help!"
"Sounds like a fun adventure!"
"Got any more of that lasagna?"

Since it was Friday, and Lyle had big family plans for the weekend, Bigfoot decided to wait until Monday to get into the first case he wanted to investigate—Clive the crow-feeder.

He checked on the progress concerning the cell phone. The forensics guy was gone for the weekend.

Bigfoot went home, grabbed his weed, a lighter, pipe and knife, and walked off into the Tillamook State Forest. He wanted a couple of days away from everything to clear his head. He had a medical marijuana card for TMJ and PTSD. But he really smoked it for its Forest Magick. No one messed with him at the station, and the chief knew he smoked it but didn't care because the weed helped chill him the fuck out.

Bigfoot went to his secret place and climbed into his tree house in one of the few remaining old cedars in the area, sixty feet above the ground. He loaded up his handmade wooden bong, sat on the edge of the platform and smoked. He thanked the marijuana for all that it did for him. He closed his eyes and saw plants waving against a clear blue sky. He followed the smoke he exhaled and drifted with it, soaking in the world around him, moving into it, diffusing.

His mind floated through the forest. He felt in touch with everything, from the most distant light of the oldest galaxy to the golden-lit moment shining off blurry dragonfly wings.

Bigfoot scratched his back on the tree. He contemplated the existence he'd carved among the humans and considered how easily it could be lost. He wondered who might miss him if he never returned to the so-called civilized world, and whom *he* might miss.

He gathered some food for the night, mostly berries and some pine needles for tea. He had some honey stashed in his Wookie house. Bigfoot had purposefully designed his tree house to resemble Chewbacca's.

Bigfoot built a big fire that night, tossing into it sage bundles, sweet-grass and cedar bark. He let the fire lull him to sleepiness. Hazy, heavy thoughts tugging him into dreams.

He spent the next day chatting with various animals who'd lived with humans and then returned to the wild—sixteen squirrels, nine chipmunks, a pigeon couple, three raccoons, a parrot, two ferrets, a deer and six crows. Many encouraged Bigfoot to forget about humans altogether.

The parrot said, "Fuck those fucking fuckholes." He'd once lived with a senator.

"I sometimes regret leaving the farm. I was safer there. Especially during hunting season," said the deer.

"I miss bread," said a pigeon.

A raccoon said, "They *do* throw out a lot of food. Campers are okay, but nothing beats dumpster diving." The other raccoons nodded and wrung their paws.

"People are terrible," said a squirrel.

"Just horrible," said another.

There was a round of squirrel-talk at that point:

"Stupid creatures."

"Mean things."

"Shouldn't be allowed to eat a single nut."

"I *need* a nut."

"Who said nut?"

The chipmunks were too busy stealing nuts from the squirrels to add much to the conversation. Except one said, "Chip and Dale are bullshit."

The ferrets were just glad to be free. They spent their days pretending to be otters, knowing well that real otters would kick their asses if they caught them doing it. They thought people should pretend to be otters. They were a bit crazy.

The crows hung-out at the tree house and got high with Bigfoot. They were more philosophical than the rest of the animals, coming from a constant lineage. The other birds were descended from dinosaurs as well, but the parrot was a drunk and the pigeons were kind of stupid.

One crow said, "You know, things come and go. Once there were no trees. One day, there will be none again. Trees do wonderful things for the planet, but it does not need them to continue its own life. Not everything loves trees. Some things hate trees. But here they are."

Another cut in, "What hates trees?"

"Ummmm…"

"Nothing hates trees," said a crow from a branch above them.

The first one said, "Shut up. Bad analogy. Whatever. Humans are fine."

"You should have used mosquitos. No one likes mosquitos."

The next morning, Bigfoot hiked upstream from the creek near his tree house along what he called Sleeping Elk Trail. It had once been a road, but a flood wiped out so much of it that it had become a sometimes narrow, sometimes non-existent path, at times leading up the mountain, and then disappearing into the boulder-strewn creek bank. The area was mostly abandoned. He rarely saw people, and because of his excellent senses, and the fact that he understood the warnings from birds and squirrels, they *never* saw him if they happened to explore beyond the designated campsites downstream.

The creek had some of the best spots in the state to find agate nodules—blue, red and clear crystal ones. Bigfoot could spend an hour searching the shallows of the creek and come away with too many gorgeous pieces of stone to carry. It was also a great place to clear his head.

Bigfoot walked nearly to the lake that fed the creek, eleven miles up from his tree house. He sat on the bank and nibbled on some mint that grew among tall grass and wet fern. He watched the water flow past rocks on its constant downhill journey. The opposite shore showed evidence of the creek's long life, water-level layers cutting a crease between mountain ridges. A seemingly endless course. An ancient pathway for countless drops of water to adventure toward the waiting sea.

A crawdad struggled against the current, picking its way around submerged rocks and digging its pointed legs into the coarse sand between them.

Bigfoot saw a glowing piece of blue agate under the crayfish. He let the little guy clamor upstream before he dug the rock out of the creek bed. No use complicating the critter's journey.

He held the agate up to the sun to see its glow.

Bigfoot sighed.

He spent the morning eating black-cap raspberries and finding agate. He thought about one day taking Syd to his tree house. Bigfoot wondered when he'd trust even the kid enough to reveal his biggest secrets to him. He considered the idea that no human could gasp their magnitude.

Chapter 6

Bigfoot walked up the dirt road toward his cabin. A white van sped around the corner, swerving into the grass to dodge him.

The van wasn't familiar to Bigfoot. Only four families lived along the road, and he tended to know the cars that came and went—even the paparazzi's. He watched it drive away. The driver tossed a lit cigarette out the window.

Bigfoot growled as he stomped the butt out and continued home.

He cut through Syd's backyard and scared the shit out of Vikki, who was sunbathing topless behind her raised pool. His shadow blocked the sun, and she opened her eyes to find him standing there, gaping at her. With a shout, she jumped out of her lawn chair.

Bigfoot signed that he was sorry and asked if Syd was home. He tried not to look at her breasts, but Vikki was bouncing around, frightened, scampering for her bikini top and spilling beer on herself.

Bigfoot thought she really was gorgeous.

Vikki signed for him to get the fuck out of there.

He did, tripping over her lawn chair and crushing it along with half of her marigold garden. She yelled in her hoarse, sexy deaf-voice and jumped up and down, signing furious swear words.

He got up and tried to apologize. She noticed him staring

at her nearly naked body and started to sign something about him being a complete pig, so he just ran away, instead.

Bigfoot took a hot shower when he got home and spent about an hour brushing his long, auburn hair. He feathered it around his head and combed straight the rest on his body.

He put his favorite song, "Handlebars" by the Flobots, on repeat on his iPod and danced around the kitchen, stuffing huge mushrooms with sage, garlic, onions and tomatoes from his indoor garden, thanking all the plants as he picked them. He popped the mushrooms in the oven and opened three root beers. Bigfoot looked through his files for Clive the red-mohawked crow-feeder on his customized computer with decent-sized keyboard. He ate a loaf of bread and two pounds of cheese while his dinner cooked.

Bigfoot texted Lyle, which was a *bitch* for him to do, and asked him to meet him in the morning at the coffee shop where Clive had last been seen—Urban Grind. It was only a few blocks from Clive's apartment. Bigfoot was hopeful that he'd been a regular there and someone could give them information that could lead to him.

After dinner, Bigfoot smoked weed on the porch while listening to the forest and watching the stars. He took a dip in his hot tub and thought more about his situation. Nearly everyone he loved was gone. The chief would be soon enough if he didn't change his habits. He thought about Syd and then Vikki. He wished he hadn't frightened her.

Bigfoot imagined himself as Vikki's boyfriend. Helping her with Syd, maybe getting her to drink less and moving them both into his place. It had been a long time since he considered sharing a home with a woman. He got out of the hot tub, brushed his hair again, searched a couple of rooms for hidden cameras and went to sleep.

He dreamt of Lara. She was dancing with him, in a green place full of sunlight and the heady scents of forest and flowers. While they spun in the ferny field, Bigfoot noticed that there were others around him. He looked up to find himself surrounded by his own kind, all dancing and rolling around in the ferns.

Bigfoot looked back to Lara. She was no longer Lara. She was a female Bigfoot. She smiled up at him and signed that she was in his heart. Her eyes drew him in. They were dark doorways. They were spirals of sinking stars. Bigfoot felt like he was on the edge of discovery. More than that, he felt electric. He felt horny. He pressed himself against the woman and she became Vikki. They fell into the ferns and Bigfoot heard the *dead words*. He awoke.

Chapter 7

Lyle and Bigfoot questioned the barista at Urban Grind. She'd served Clive on the day he'd disappeared. She said he was nice, and yes, he'd been in a few times before. No, she didn't know anything about him. Yes, he seemed happy. No, he didn't say anything about where he was going. No one had met him. Nothing suspicious had happened. He'd walked up the block when he left.

Bigfoot had Lyle ask if there were any bigger cups for coffee and get the biggest one they had, but it still looked tiny in his hand.

Lyle was discouraged and didn't know why Bigfoot had chosen this case to start the day, especially since he seemed to have a soft spot for the missing kids. Bigfoot didn't answer, but asked instead if Lyle had learned anything from Clive's work associates.

"I got nothin'," Lyle said.

Bigfoot suggested they walk down the same street Clive had.

Lyle sneezed. He said, "Look, I really need to go. My daughter's robot-fighting match is at three, and it's nearly eleven already. I'll probably run into traffic."

Bigfoot prodded him down the sidewalk.

A homeless woman, wearing three ratty sweaters, picked at her long, gray hair and lounged under the freeway overpass. Bigfoot had Lyle ask if she stayed there often.

"Yeah," she said, scratching her head. "Most every day."

Lyle asked about Clive. Bigfoot showed her a photo on his phone, which was a *bitch* for him to use.

"Oh, yeah. I seen him several times. Hard to miss with his hair and all. Sometimes he gives me smokes when he come past. He gotta live close by."

Lyle said, "Too bad he didn't give you soap."

Bigfoot frowned at him. The woman was putrid, certainly. She smelled like rotten potatoes, but somehow worse, with an unpleasant undertone of skunk. But there was no reason to say so. He wrote some things down for Lyle to ask.

She thought she'd seen Clive on the day he disappeared, but wasn't sure. "Is he okay?" she asked.

Lyle said, "Well, he's, uh, *missing*."

"Oh, yeah. Missin'. My cat is missin'. I'm sure the van-man took her. If I ever see him again, I'm throwin' this jar of pee on 'im!" She pulled a yellow jar out of one of the pockets of her filth-smeared cargo pants and shook it at them. "Got a smoke, or five bucks or somethin'?"

Bigfoot gave her ten.

Lyle left for his daughter's robot fight.

Bigfoot went back to the station to piece together what he knew. It wasn't much. He thought maybe he'd started with the wrong case. But when crows were concerned about something, it was usually important. Though frustrated, Bigfoot decided to stick with Clive. Later, he checked with forensics and learned that the phone had no prints but his own.

He drove home. Vikki sat on his porch. Bigfoot was glad she hadn't tried to get inside the cabin. After finding the cameras, he'd set traps whenever he left it.

Her face was flushed, and her thick mascara had melted down her cheeks. She jumped up as he pulled into the driveway and ran to meet him. He had no choice but watch her breasts bounce in her short, tight shirt. They nearly fell out the bottom of the ragged fabric, which had been cut across the base of the red #10 printed on the front.

Bigfoot was glad he wore pants, or what remained of them, as he climbed out of his truck. He concentrated on watching Vikki's hands as she signed.

"Syd's missing! Since yesterday. Probably before you... came by," she said. "It's not that weird for him to take off, but he always comes home by dark, and he was supposed to be mowing the lawn. I must have fallen asleep watching TV while I waited for him. He wasn't home when I woke up. I've looked everywhere, and I'm really freaking out and I need your help."

Bigfoot investigated Syd's house.

He found the mower just outside the garage. The gas cap was off. A can of gasoline sat beside it.

Vikki brought him a root beer. He was surprised that she knew what he drank.

Bigfoot looked around. He saw a squirrel and asked her if she'd been around the day before.

The squirrel said, "Yep. This is my tree. I know Syd. He's never thrown a rock at me, always gives me nuts. Yep, Syd. Good kid. But that Tate. He's a little dick. Drives that loud motorcycle around and slingshots pellets at all of us.

He's a rotten, little animal. Syd got into a van with Tate yesterday. Drove off. That Tate McWillis. He sucks."

Bigfoot knew Tate. He was a wild one. Always getting into mischief. He'd nearly destroyed Bigfoot's garden the summer before while riding his loud little dirt bike through his yard. Bigfoot thought about Tate being a redhead.

When he asked for further details, the squirrel said a cloud decal was on the back of the van. "It was hard to see, because it was white, but the bottom had a shadow."

Bigfoot thanked the squirrel and examined the tire tracks in the dirt road. He wished he knew as much about tires as he did hooves, claws and feet.

Bigfoot signed to Vikki that he'd do whatever was necessary to find Syd. He told her what the squirrel had said. She looked at him like he was crazy before going inside to change her clothes.

Vikki asked Bigfoot to stay at the station. She had to fill out paperwork and talk to investigators. Bigfoot explained the situation to Lieutenant Jacobi and found a female officer who spoke sign language to stay with Vikki. He had paperwork to fill out, too.

Tate's parents arrived. They'd called the day before, when Tate didn't come home for dinner, and had been notified when Bigfoot reported Syd missing, too. They'd both been crying. An officer took statements from them and gathered photos and other information about their son.

Luckily, the chief knew that it wasn't bullshit that Bigfoot could talk to animals—he'd seen him do it countless times. He *did* think it was a little coincidental that Bigfoot had just been assigned to the Missing Persons Unit when a friend of his went missing. But Bigfoot said it was the way nature worked.

The chief said, "If there's a goddamn witness to the boys being abducted, they aren't missing, they're kidnapped, and other officers will be in charge of that sort of investigation. But first we need some other evidence besides the word of a goddamn squirrel. That might be enough for you and me, but I can't mobilize a goddamn detective unit based on information from a goddamn tree-rat."

Bigfoot grumbled.

"I know how you feel about the boy, and while it isn't the best goddamn idea to have you out there working a case like this, I can't just tell you to ignore it. Besides, I just had this goddamn office remodeled. I don't need you goin' on a goddamn rampage. Get me some goddamn evidence, and I'll put everyone I can on it."

Bigfoot texted Lyle to meet him at the freeway underpass to question the homeless lady about her missing cat.

Chapter 8

Bigfoot handed the woman a ten-dollar bill. She told him that his pants were ripped. It happened every time he sat in one of those tiny sedans.

Lyle asked the woman about the man who'd stolen her cat.

"The dude in the van. He's always cruisin' around here real slow—just about every day. Like he's lookin' for somethin'. Ol' Ronnie says he got a bad feeling about that van. An' Ronnie's feelins is usually dead-on. Last week I seen the van-man parked right here as I was comin' back up the street from the park—got two hotdogs from this fat kid, and I was gonna share with Shadow. But she din't come when I called her. And she ain't shown up since. I know he took her. I'm gonna throw pee on him."

Lyle rolled his eyes, put his little notebook away and mumbled something about bums.

Bigfoot wrote in his notebook. He showed it to Lyle.

Lyle asked the lady, "What color is the van?"

"White."

Again, Bigfoot showed what he'd written to his partner.

Lyle said, "No fuckin' way."

There was a single word on the page: STAKEOUT

Bigfoot nodded at the woman and said, "Thaaanks." He walked toward the coffee shop into a gritty, misty rain.

Lyle caught up with him. "I didn't know you could talk."

Bigfoot just shook his head. He could only say a few

words, and they sounded gruff and scary when he did, so he usually didn't. Mostly he grunted, growled, cooed, clicked, whistled, laughed and grumbled. Unless he yelled, "HAAALT!" at suspects, which scared the shit out them. Sometimes literally.

Bigfoot told Lyle about the white van while they had coffee at Urban Grind. He explained how they would wait until they saw the van and follow it. Simple enough.

Lyle said, "It seems you're onto something with the van. But seriously, there are a lot of white vans in and around the city. And the chief told me to keep you under control. Like *that's* possible. But still, a stakeout isn't exactly keeping you off the street."

Bigfoot shrugged. He wanted to be low-key, but was worried about the boys. Especially Syd.

Lyle asked, "When do we start?"

Bigfoot wrote, NOW.

Lyle protested. "I have to get home. Monday night is fried chicken and mashed potatoes night, you know. Trish has already put it off. The game started half an hour ago, and I have to take the trash to the curb. You should go back to the station and check out how many white vans there are in the city, coordinate with the officers in the MPU and see if we can maybe get a better description of the van to narrow down that list."

Bigfoot nodded and wrote: How did robot fighting go? Did your daughter do well?

Lyle smiled. "Her team won."

Vikki was still at the station. When Bigfoot asked her why, she signed, "Waiting for you."

Bigfoot checked with the lieutenant and explained that he and Lyle would be on stakeout. He filled out paperwork and read an email from forensics stating that the phone he'd discovered had been purchased from a kiosk at the train station. No surveillance of the purchase.

He took Vikki home in his monster truck.

She invited him inside.

He ducked through the door. It was a lot less messy than the last time he'd visited her trailer. Of course, there had been parties going on just about every other time.

"Want a drink?"

Bigfoot signed, "Root beer."

"With vodka?"

Bigfoot shook his head. He sat on the floor near the dining table. The floor creaked.

He watched Vikki in the kitchen. She'd changed into jeans and a full t-shirt when they left for the station. Absentmindedly, he recalled the bottoms of her breasts falling out of the shirt she'd worn earlier.

She brought Bigfoot a root beer before making a vodka and tonic for herself. She sat at the table beside him.

Bigfoot asked, "Was Syd upset yesterday? Did something happen?"

Vikki shook her head dismissively. "No."

"No fights?"

She frowned. "What do you mean?"

He shrugged.

Vikki sat up straight. "No. What do you mean?"

"Syd has mentioned that you and your boyfriends argue, and it sometimes involves Syd. He gets pretty upset."

Vikki narrowed her eyes and took a drink. "Nothing like that."

Bigfoot finished his root beer in a gulp. "Okay."

Vikki signed angrily, "You know, that's bullshit. Blaming me for my son being kidnapped." She started crying. She chugged the rest of her tall drink.

Bigfoot told her, "I didn't mean that at all. I just—"

Vikki slapped his huge hands. She pointed at the door. He got up and walked gingerly to it.

Vikki wasn't looking at him. She sat at the table, still crying.

Bigfoot waited until she looked up. "I'll talk to you tomorrow," he signed.

She flipped him off.

Chapter 9

Bigfoot and Lyle staked out the underpass in Bigfoot's truck.

Lyle said, "I don't know how inconspicuous we are in a huge blue monster truck with flames and shit all over it."

Bigfoot ignored him. He'd had enough of being cramped in a car.

They took turns going for coffee and pastries. Bigfoot brought a mug from home, which held nearly a full pot of coffee. He'd sculpted it in pottery class when he was twelve. Holding it made him happy.

The first day passed with no vans. Lyle played *Angry Birds* on his phone and talked about his wife's cooking and where he was going to fly-fish after he retired. Bigfoot thought most of the places sounded nice—Harriman State Park in Idaho, Ochoco Reservoir in Central Oregon, The Grand Canyon, a float trip down the Salmon River and a lake in Belgium. Lyle often texted his wife as well, but wasn't sneezing as much as he usual did

Bigfoot watched people. He counted how many of them were kind to the homeless folks along the underpass, how many ignored them, and how many were mean or snickered to their friends.

The majority ignored them.

Vikki was at Bigfoot's desk when they arrived back at the station. She looked more put-together than usual. Sexy still, but less wild and disheveled.

She signed, "Hi. I thought I'd stop in and see if you found anything out."

"Sorry. Nothing."

Vikki looked at the floor.

Bigfoot waved his hand in her line of sight. He signed, "How did you get here?"

"My friend gave me a ride. I've been here for a couple of hours."

"Would you like a ride home?"

She nodded. "Can we get some dinner first?"

Natasha, the girl working at Sizzle Pie, smiled when Bigfoot entered. She said, "Usual?"

Bigfoot nodded. He led Vikki to a table near the window. He liked to watch who went into Powell's Books.

Vikki asked, "What did you order?"

"Large *Total Jammer* pizza with tomatoes, onions and roasted garlic. Lots of root beer. Is that okay?"

"Sure."

Bigfoot signed, "I'm sorry about yesterday. I didn't mean to say that I blamed you."

"Oh, don't worry. I know. I thought about it. I'm sorry for being so mean to you. It's just... I feel like screaming."

Bigfoot nodded.

They looked out the windows for a while. Then Vikki signed, "I'm going crazy. If we don't find Syd soon, I'm going to start knocking on every door in the city. I want him home. Every day I feel emptier. I'm sure he's alive. I'd know if he wasn't."

"I know, Vikki. I do, too. I won't stop until I find him. I wish we had more to go on. But we'll get him back."

Vikki took his hand. She could only really hold his thumb and forefinger. She gripped them tight.

Bigfoot squeezed lightly. He hoped it hadn't hurt her.

Her eyes were wet and glowing. Lights reflected in them, reminding Bigfoot of his dream.

They finally broke eye contact when a skateboarder ground past and thudded against the window. Bigfoot noted the line of Vikki's neck and how smooth her skin was, stretched over her collarbone.

Natasha arrived with the pizza and two pitchers of root beer.

Bigfoot asked Vikki, "Do you want a beer?"

She shook her head. "No, root beer, please."

Bigfoot half-smiled. He wrote her order on his notebook and showed it to Natasha.

Vikki asked, "So, you come here often?"

Bigfoot nodded and loaded a slice onto her plate. He ate a piece and took another.

Vikki laughed, bit into her pizza and then signed, "Bigfoot, how did you get here? I mean, why are you a cop? Why aren't you living in the woods?"

"I do live in the woods."

"You know what I mean. I want to know why you're here."

"That's a long story."

"We have plenty of pizza." She smiled. "As long as you take it easy."

Trying not to show his teeth, Bigfoot smiled, too. He ate another slice of pizza and signed, "I'm sure you've heard the story of how I was saved from poachers."

Vikki nodded. "But never from you."

Natasha brought Vikki's root beer.

"Well, it all happened fast. My mom was killed in front of me. Cassidy found me, and I went home with him. When he spoke to me, it was the first human voice I'd ever heard, but it sounded kind and Cassidy felt like a good person. Still, I was in shock.

"At his house, I realized that everything had changed—*everything*—in about a second. I considered running away, but I also didn't want to be alone. The chief's wife Brenda—she's dead now—brought me a stuffed toy alligator. I guess it was all she could find in a hurry. I'd never seen anything like it and thought it was a dead animal at first. Later, she brought me a bear."

"How did you communicate?"

Bigfoot laughed. "Really bad sign language. Pointing and nodding, mostly."

"I know what that's like."

"I'm sure." He ate a slice of pizza.

Vikki ate some of hers.

Bigfoot signed, "So they made me comfortable, fed me whatever I pointed at, and Brenda sat with me when I cried. The chief took photos. You can imagine their excitement and concern."

"Yes. I'm sorry, but I would have been freaking out."

"Oh, they were. We all were. They decided to go as public as possible to protect me. But they were careful about things. Of course, I barely knew what was happening at that point. After a barrage of TV, magazine and news reporters, scientific investigations, medical examinations, zoological presentations, government evaluations, intelligence tests and consent for surveillance, Cassidy adopted me.

"I was privately tutored for a year before they put me in school. I learned ASL quickly, having signed my people's language for years. But I was definitely freaking out the whole time—the tests, the government, the media... It was almost too much. My only friends were the chief and his wife. They came to see me every day, and I grew to love them nearly as much as I did my new dad. Brenda even learned to sign. I had no idea there was a media-storm surrounding me, and assumed that everyone had to wrestle past crowds of people at their front doors." Bigfoot sipped root beer. "Are you sure you want me to explain all this?"

Vikki put a slice of pizza on her plate and wiped her hands. She signed, "I do."

"I mean, I know you've got a lot on your mind."

"This helps me feel better." She took another bite. "Please, tell me more."

Bigfoot signed, "I started private school in the third grade at *The Pye School*—P-Y-E, but the kids called it, *Pie School*. They called *me* lots of things—Furby, Chewbacca, Big Ass, Monkey Boy and Apey-Face. School was bad for me from the start. The largest uniform didn't fit, and the stupid beret looked like a flat licorice jellybean on my head. My hair stuck out from under it like a porcupine on its back. My pants always ripped and my ass would hang out. I fought a lot. I always won, but I always held back, too. I knew I could tear any of those kids to pieces with minimal effort. But I also knew I'd never be accepted if I showed my true strength."

Vikki sucked on her straw. Bigfoot was happy she liked root beer. "I'm sure you could have killed any them. I've seen the news."

Bigfoot looked at his plate and nodded slowly.

Vikki waved at him until he looked back up. "I don't blame you. I'd rip off those assholes' arms if I could, too. I like that you're here, protecting us."

"Thank you. You know I'll do anything to find Syd, right?"

"I know. Yes."

They ate pizza for a few minutes, then Vikki said, "I've seen plenty about you on TV. That's why I'm asking this stuff. I remember growing up and hearing about you, and it not being that big of a deal until I was older. I mean, everyone's interested in you." She looked outside at the people who passed them. "I imagine it's been really hard."

"It's been good and bad, and like you said, pretty public. I made appearances on talk shows, had news crews and paparazzi follow me around, was pestered by anthropologists, creationists, members of the various religions that formed around me, and Bigfoot hunters looking for more of my kind. I did what I could to tolerate it.

"I volunteered at the animal shelter, worked on a local farm, tutored kids in math, natural sciences and history. I was in the Chess Club. The Boy Scouts wouldn't let me join, so I haunted their outings for years, scaring some kids so badly that they never went camping again. But I never made a lot of friends. Luckily, I had my dad."

"You terrorized Boy Scouts?"

Bigfoot tried to read Vikki's expression. "Well, most of them were kids from school who teased me."

Vikki smiled. "I like you."

He returned the smile before offering her the last slice of pizza.

She declined and said, "Your dad seems like he was a pretty amazing guy."

"He really was great. He cared for me but never sheltered me, except to keep me safe from exploitation. One of the saddest things I've seen in this world is that many people don't have good relationships with their fathers."

"Yeah." Vikki looked outside at the charcoal dusk reflected in the shoe store's windows across the street. Then she signed, "I don't want to be rude, but I'm pretty wiped out. That pizza was great, but eating made me sleepy. Can you take me home?"

"Of course."

They sat parked in Vikki's driveway for a few minutes. Finally, Vikki faced him. She stroked his arm and signed, "I'm sorry it took Syd being missing for me to ask about you. I think I just wanted to trust you more. I mean, I know you're Syd's friend. I just... I'm not sure what I mean. I like you, Bigfoot. Thank you for everything." She hugged him, jumped down from the truck and walked to her trailer, turning once to wave.

Chapter 10

"So what's up with the kid's mom? Got somethin' goin' on there, Big Guy?" Lyle asked the next morning while he climbed into Bigfoot's monster truck.

Bigfoot shrugged and sipped from his giant mug.

"Come on," Lyle said. "Spill it."

Bigfoot wrote in his notebook: We had pizza. I took her home and came back here.

"Wait. You've been here all night?"

He nodded.

"Then you should get some sleep." Lyle pulled out his phone.

Bigfoot looked at the phone and shook his head.

"Okay. I'll keep a lookout." Lyle tucked the phone away. "You rest."

Bigfoot crossed his arms and let his head fall. He was asleep in under a minute. Again, he dreamt of his people dancing, but now Taliban soldiers attacked them. His kind ran from the slaughter, but none escaped. The Sasquatch Hunter stepped from clouds of smoke that clogged the fern forest. He held eight chains in his hand, each connected to shackles around the necks of his rabid, gnashing zombie brothers—the men Bigfoot had killed.

Lyle tapped Bigfoot's hairy arm. "Action, Big Guy."

Bigfoot jerked awake. He hit the dashboard and dented it. He growled.

"Careful!"

The detectives were parked up the street, near a cab company. Bigfoot looked in the rearview mirror at the van in the shadow of the overpass. A driver and a passenger were visible. The van crept along the curb.

Homeless people lounged in a row along the fence bordering the sidewalk. Most ignored the van. The cat lady didn't. She jumped up from her tattered blanket, threw something at the passenger window and broke it. The van took off, speeding straight past Bigfoot and Lyle.

Bigfoot followed it. He saw a cloud decal on its back door.

Lyle radioed dispatch with the van's license plate number. "She threw a jar of pee at him!" he shouted.

Bigfoot parked as the van drove inside a warehouse.

The dispatcher announced, "The van is registered to the Silver Linings Chemical Disposal Company. They have ten white vans registered."

Bigfoot growled.

Lyle thanked the dispatcher.

They sat and watched the building.

Lyle said, "We should go back to the station and check out the company. I doubt that it has anything to do with abducting children. It's probably a driver cruising for a hooker over anything shadier."

Bigfoot agreed to do some research on the company and its employees. He wrote: I know we don't have much to go on, but I want to follow this lead, even if it seems like it came from nowhere. I trust my instincts.

Lyle said, "I trust your end stinks, too." He laughed.

Bigfoot coordinated with the lieutenant and told Lyle to go home. He learned that Silver Linings, once a family-run business, had recently been sold. The new owner, Lance Parfait, had fired and replaced the entire staff—including the grandson, two nephews, a great-niece and the great-granddaughter of the founder.

Lance Parfait owned several businesses in various fields—a microbiology lab, a chemical food-additive research and development facility, a sports medicine franchise, three different tour companies operating on nearly every continent of the world, a genetic library and testing lab, an airline, a mining tools company, steel mill, nature preserve, wilderness survival school, robotics manufacturing company and a private anthropology college, among other eclectic businesses, grants, fellowships and memberships to think-tanks and an archeological society. He'd even written an autobiography, and he was only in his forties. He didn't seem like the kidnapping type.

Though, if Lance Parfait was as smart and benevolent as he appeared, how had he managed to hire a kidnapper who used his company vans to swipe people off the street? Or maybe *he* was the kidnapper. Or perhaps the abductor was someone who had previously worked for the company. Or they'd sold a van to someone… Plenty of leads needed to be investigated, but Bigfoot's intuition told him that Silver Linings was the place to start looking.

Vikki sat slumped on his porch when he arrived home. She'd been crying. The paparazzi hadn't tired of taking photos of her from the road. They had cameras that could focus on the freckles on her clavicle from five hundred feet away. Bigfoot parked so that his truck was in their line of sight. No paparazzi ever went to the back or side of his house. Not since the "backyard incident."

Vikki signed, "I haven't heard anything all day."

"I have a lead, but nothing solid yet. Please, come inside,"

In the living room, Bigfoot took off his shirt and tie. He hated wearing clothes, but decided to keep his pants on. Not *all* the seams had been torn.

He started a fire, opted not to put on any music, and sat Vikki down on a barstool across from the rock countertop in the kitchen where he made dinner.

She watched him cut peppers for quesadillas. "Are you vegetarian?"

Bigfoot explained that he'd never had the desire to eat meat. "It would be difficult for anyone to eat animals if they could speak with them the way I do."

Vikki said that it made his teeth seem less scary.

"What would you like to drink? I have root beer, sage tea, lemonade or water. No alcohol."

"Root beer. No, sage tea. Can I have both? I quit drinking alcohol."

"So that's why you didn't order a beer at Sizzle Pie."

Vikki smiled.

Bigfoot brought her drinks then returned to putting together the quesadillas. He chopped and grated while Vikki looked around at the stuff in his house. She was drawn particularly to the immense rock fireplace in the living room—it was built with huge chunks of glowing agate interspersed with granite blocks. She had to look over a hand-carved maple dining room table to see it.

Bigfoot was looking at *her* when she spun the barstool back around.

"Your couches are huge," she signed.

They ate at the dining room table. Bigfoot piled some pillows on Vikki's chair so she sat at a comfortable level. He watched her take a bite of quesadilla. Her lips were like some sweet fruit, pink and glistening. He noticed how her nipples pressed against her t-shirt.

Vikki chewed and signed, "Syd told me you have a hot tub. Is it oversized, like everything else?"

"Yes. I carved it out of granite—sized for me. But I made benches that are comfortable for humans." He couldn't stop looking at her breasts.

"I'll bet it's nice."

Bigfoot met her stare. She half-smiled, like she knew that he'd been picturing her sliding naked into the tub. Bigfoot's throbbing dick ripped his pants. He excused himself and crept awkwardly from the dining room to the bathroom. He suspected Vikki knew what had happened.

When he returned, wearing new pants, she was nearly done eating. He made coffee to avoid staring at her body while she talked to him. He wanted to be compassionate, to just be a friend for her. It was hard, because signing not only drew attention to her breasts, but Vikki was also an animated speaker.

He led her to the living room and sat on a couch near the fireplace.

Vikki said, "On TV they say that if they don't find an abducted person in the first twenty-four hours, they're not likely to ever find that person. It's been four days."

He knew the statistics. Bigfoot told her that he and the other policemen were doing their job the best they could. He said, "Once the rest of the force admits that the boys have been abducted, I could be taken off the case. But I'll work to prove that they were kidnapped, and I'll do whatever it takes to find them, even if I'm not officially assigned to the case."

Vikki hopped up on the couch. Her legs stuck out at a crazy angle, like a little kid on regular-sized furniture. "I miss him so much. I can't work. I don't do much but wait for him to walk through the door."

"He will. I'll find him, Vikki. Soon."

"I know you will. Really, I'm sure of it." She stared at the fireplace.

Bigfoot reached over and added a few thick logs to the fire. He felt her watch him. The picture he'd constructed of her in the hot tub lingered like an image from a photoflash—superimposed on the following moments, clearly visible behind closed eyes. Bigfoot shut his eyes.

She sat with her legs crossed when he turned around.

They sipped coffee for a few minutes.

Vikki placed her coffee cup between her legs to sign. "Tell me more about you growing up."

Bigfoot knew that she just needed to talk about something other than her missing son. If he was worried about Syd, he could imagine how it consumed her. She needed to be reassured, but also needed to be distracted. Not only that, she seemed genuinely interested.

He sipped from his huge mug and set it on the side table. "I told you about school."

"Yes. And then you joined the Army?"

"I did. When I was eighteen. I wanted to do something to make my dad proud. But I also wanted to escape the prodding and poking. Get away from celebrity and maybe see more of the world. I knew I'd get to learn more about humans—though I'd seen enough about them to make me wonder sometimes if I wanted to see more. But I actually enjoyed the Army and being a soldier. Eventually, I earned a place in the Rangers."

Sipping coffee, Vikki looked up at him. She raised her eyebrows.

He nodded. "I went to war and learned all I needed to know about people and the rest of the world. The upside to enlisting was that once I was in the service, no one could fuck with me. Well, no one but the Army. I also learned that being shot by most guns didn't hurt me. The downside was...well, war."

"Being shot doesn't hurt you?"

"I was hit several times by an AK-47 during a firefight and barely felt a sting. So I tested out a few other weapons. Only the higher caliber rounds did any sort of damage, with fifty caliber rounds barely bruising me. My buddies had fun shooting at my ass. I knew that a shot to the eye or ear would kill me—my mother had been hit in the ear, and my real father had speared himself through the eye and died a year before her in a freak accident involving elk antlers, a dead frog and psychedelic mushrooms."

"No wonder you always catch the bad guys." She watched Bigfoot drink coffee and squirm uncomfortably. "So, you became a cop because of your dad."

Bigfoot put his mug down. "I was on a mission in the mountains of Afghanistan when he was killed trying to stop a junkie from robbing the little grocery store around the corner from his house. My dad was off-duty, and only wearing a jogging suit. He threw bottles of beer at the robber when he aimed to shoot the clerk. My dad was shot, and the junkie was never caught. I learned about it three weeks later."

"I'm sorry. If you don't want to talk about it—"

Bigfoot kept signing. "His death hit me hard, and after the only drinking binge in my life, I went on a rampage through the mountains of Afghanistan. I wiped out some key installations and a few platoons of soldiers before I got my head straight. They awarded me medals and commendations and all that crap that I didn't give a shit about anymore because I just wanted the one human in the world who'd ever come close to understanding me. I was discharged six months after my dad died."

Vikki put her hand on Bigfoot's knee.

"Once I got out of the Army, my celebrity had faded a bit. Gun-control riots, the Big Quake, Assball, the Anti-Christ Pope and Shark Chupacabra had replaced me. I was okay with that. After a year of island-hopping, port-city partying and an Icelandic expedition to the best hot springs I've found in the world, I joined the police force. I decided that I'd devote the rest of my life to punishing people like the junkie who killed my dad." Bigfoot looked at Vikki's hand on his knee. He hadn't realized she'd put it there. It was tiny, warm and electric.

She moved it to sign, "Damn."

"Yeah," Bigfoot signed. "Damn."

They sat and finished their coffees.

Vikki stood. "Thank you for dinner. And for telling me this stuff."

"My pleasure, Vikki. But next time it's my turn to learn more about you."

She smiled. "Next time."

"I'll find Syd," he signed.

"I know you will."

Vikki hugged him. She ran her fingers through the long hair on his lower back. He was glad his singed hair was already re-growing.

He watched her walk away.

Bigfoot smoked from his massive bong. He went outside and tossed pebbles into the sky to be mistaken for insects by bats. The rocks thudded on the grass and plinked into the creek. Bigfoot knew that the longer he waited, the more difficult it would be to find the boys. He decided to deviate from procedure.

Bigfoot jumped into his monster truck and drove to the Silver Linings warehouse.

There was no point in waiting for evidence to walk outside the warehouse door while Syd and Tate spent another night missing. Bigfoot used shadow-skills to avoid security cameras and broke into the place by leaping to an open window fifteen feet above the ground. No alarms sounded when he climbed inside.

He jumped into an open room where seven vans were parked. Bigfoot investigated them, sniffing each one for signs of the boys. He smelled plenty of people's scents in the vans, but not Syd or Tate's. He found the one with the broken window.

Bigfoot entered the offices situated about the parking bay.

In the first, Syd's favorite knife sat on the desk beside a hula-dancer bobblehead. Bigfoot knew the knife immediately. He didn't have to examine it for the *S* carved into the hilt. Bigfoot sniffed the knife and smelled human blood that had been washed clean. It wasn't Syd's blood. Bigfoot replaced the knife. He searched the rest of the warehouse and found no evidence of foul play or kidnapped children.

He tried to use a computer in one of the bigger offices, but the keyboard was too small and he needed a password. He accidentally broke the mouse.

Bigfoot left the warehouse, all the while working on a plan to obtain a search warrant.

He spent a restless few hours in his hammock.

Chapter 11

Before work, Bigfoot went to Washington Park to talk to the crows. He had a plan to use them to watch all of the Silver Linings vans and let him know when any of the drivers did something illegal, especially if it involved kidnapping. The crows agreed to this.

When Bigfoot arrived at the station, the chief called him into his office. "The goddamn vice-president of Silver Linings Chemical Disposal stopped by first thing this morning with his security chief and goddamn company lawyers. They showed me some video from their goddamn warehouse recorded last night."

Bigfoot shuffled his feet, knocking over a chair that slid into the chief's coffee bar. It spilled hot coffee, creamer, wet grounds, sugar, and broke two mugs.

The chief yelled, "BigfoooOOOOooooot!"

Bigfoot tried to clean the mess.

"Leave it! Just. Just leave it. Bigfoot, you know how bad you fucked up. You're not only off this case—you're suspended until you appear before a review board."

Bigfoot wrote in his notebook. You can't, chief! Syd's knife was in that warehouse. We have to get a warrant and search them. We need to go through their files. We need to investigate their employees. And Lance Parfait!

The chief glanced at Bigfoot's message. "Do you know what it took to keep you from being *arrested*? Not to mention the goddamn strings I had to pull and promises I had to make so they wouldn't goddamn sue us. You know I bend over backward for you, and not just because you're like my goddamn family. I know you're good at your job. But this isn't like accidentally pulling the arms off some goddamn bad guy who deserves it. I can't make this go away."

Bigfoot looked down at the chief. He snatched his notebook and pointed at the part about Syd's knife.

"You're suspended, Bigfoot. I need your badge and your gun. And if you go within a hundred yards of that goddamn warehouse, Lance goddamn Parfait, or any of those goddamn white vans, I *will* have you arrested."

Bigfoot made fists and growled, "Chieeeeeeef!"

"Get out of my office. Go to the mountains. We'll find the kid." The chief held out his hands. "I'm also taking the cost to replace their goddamn computer mouse out of your pay."

Begrudgingly, Bigfoot surrendered his gun and badge. He stalked out of the office, tearing the new carpet behind him and ripping the door off its hinges. Storming past Lyle, he snatched the donut from his hand.

Bigfoot wanted to throw cars, pull up street signs, rip off some arms, or stomp the whole city down. Instead, he drove his monster truck back home. There, he took off his crappy suit, uprooted a couple of trees, threw some boulders, drank a cup of tea and smoked a huge joint.

He realized that he rarely pulled his gun or showed his badge. Being suspended didn't mean he couldn't still look for Syd and Tate. When it really came down to it, who would stop him?

Bigfoot walked to Vikki's.

She answered the door, wearing only a t-shirt and panties. Bigfoot picked her up and carried her to bed. He tore off her shirt and sucked one of her breasts almost entirely into his mouth. He licked her from her neck to the elastic band of her underwear, which he ripped off with his teeth. He beheld her gorgeous, squirming body. Her nipples were the same shade of pink as her lips, and between her legs, under glistening blonde pubic hair, he saw that pink shine, too.

She lifted her hips, shifted the weight of her breasts, widened the spread of her legs and tightened her stomach.

He bent to taste her. Vikki seized handfuls of Bigfoot's long shoulder-hair and rode his long, thick tongue. She came twice, and the bed broke before she couldn't take it anymore and yanked on his hair to make him stop lapping at her.

His gigantic, hard dick was intimidating, fascinatingly hairless and a huge turn-on. Vikki skittered down the slanted mattress and inserted its head between her lips. She couldn't take much more into her mouth, but she slurped and licked and rubbed her hands all over it.

Bigfoot cooed and groaned. He stroked Vikki's corn-silk hair and tickled her nipples. He pulled his cock from her mouth, stood, picked her up and slid his dick between her legs so that she straddled it.

Balancing with her hands on Bigfoot's shoulders, Vikki put all of her weight on his cock. She slid back and forth on it, coming again. Bigfoot slipped Vikki onto her feet and lay on his back. She climbed onto him.

Vikki took Bigfoot into her as far as she was able. She gasped and pulled on his chest hair as they fucked.

Bigfoot struggled to hold back his orgasm; he hadn't had sex in three years. He'd fantasized about Vikki being wrapped around him for quite some time, and she was even sexier and sweeter than he'd imagined—her hair, her shining eyes, her bouncing tits on his belly, her pussy holding him so tight. He squeezed one of her perfect ass-cheeks and pushed himself a little deeper. Vikki squealed, pounded on his chest and came again.

Bigfoot pulled Vikki off of him. Sitting her on her ass between his legs, he painted her with his semen. A spurt of the stuff shot over her head and knocked a lamp off the nightstand on the other side of the broken bed. Vikki shouted with laughter and wiped the cum from her eyes. Then she led him to the tiny shower.

After they were clean, they sat and shared a joint. Bigfoot told Vikki that he'd been suspended.

"What?!"

"It's okay. It actually means I can look for Syd without following police procedure. I'm thinking of quitting, anyway. I always get knocked down for not following the rules. I want to help people and uphold the law, but there are too many restrictions. Following the rules, in this case, would mean abandoning my friend. That isn't going to happen."

Pushing her tongue between his teeth, Vikki kissed Bigfoot.

Chapter 12

Bigfoot drove to Powell's and bought Lance Parfait's book. He took it to Washington Park and sat under a tree near the playground.

The crows didn't have any new information. They'd been following vans, but nothing weird had gone down.

Bigfoot read Parfait's autobiography. The guy, it seemed, was a conceited fuckhead. He went on and on throughout the book about how smart he was and how the rest of academia were idiots and robots. But there were some interesting things in it, too, like his ideas about ancient civilizations and the ruins from which he drew his unique conclusions—Baalbek, Saqqara, Aztlan and hidden Inca cities.

His phone rang. It was Lyle. "What the hell? I've called you fifteen times since you left."

Bigfoot growled.

"I'm sorry about your suspension, but what were you thinking? Look, how about coming over to my place for dinner tonight? It's Taco Night. My daughter's a vegetarian, so there's stuff for you weirdos, too."

Bigfoot looked around the park. He watched kids on a seesaw. "'Kaaaaay," he said.

"Good," said Lyle. "See you at six."

As soon as he hung up, his phone rang again. He answered without checking the caller, assuming Lyle had called back.

But it wasn't Lyle. "Suspended, eh? You bad boy. What are we going to do with you?" It was the man who'd called from outside his cabin. The one who'd bugged him.

Bigfoot said, "Raaaaaahhhhhhhhh!"

"Meet me at the zoo. Black Bear Ridge." The man hung up.

Bigfoot stood and surveyed the area. A few people were talking on their phones. A couple of kids were texting or playing games. No one looked suspicious. A few people close to him appeared nervous, having heard his reply to the caller. They watched him search the crowd.

He strode quiet forest trails toward the zoo just over the hill. He considered having the number traced but knew it would be fruitless. Clearly, he was dealing with a professional.

Bigfoot smelled oncoming rain. The ferns were curling slightly, bending in anticipation of a downpour. Moss glowed, and the dark soil reddened nearly imperceptivity. Just through the trees, the tops of condos were visible. Stark and unchanging, they contrasted sharply with the things of nature.

He thought about living away from people again. He wondered if Vikki and Syd would join him in the wilderness. Syd would. He thought about his dream, spinning with Lara, then a Bigfoot woman, and then Vikki. He wondered who was messing with him. And why.

He jumped the twenty-foot-tall fence into the zoo at the elephant enclosure. It was being remodeled. The plan was to give the elephants "more space to roam."

Bigfoot thought for the millionty-fifth time about smashing all the fences and doors in the zoo and giving *all* the animals more space to roam.

He passed the oldest elephant in the hodgepodge zoo family. "Hey, Stampy," he said.

"Whistler," the elephant replied, munching grass.

Bigfoot jumped to the roof of the elephant building, where they locked them up at night and "kept them warm" in winter. He double-flipped from that over the wall of the outer enclosure and onto the walkway. People watched him, of course. They murmured to one another about why Bigfoot was in the elephant cage. Tourists snapped photos. Mostly, he ignored them, but gently high-fived a kid in a wheelchair who smiled lopsidedly at him with his hand raised.

He arrived at the bear habitat. The black bear couple had recently had three cubs. The smallest, a girl with duff-colored fur, reared up and greeted him. "Bigfoot! Berries?"

"Not today, Junie," he said.

Her brothers emerged from their tiny fiberglass cave to greet Bigfoot, but didn't bother to ask for berries, having heard his reply. They waved and wrestled each other.

Bigfoot's phone rang.

"I have a deal for you, Bigfoot. I just want a blood sample. If you give me some of your blood, I'll consider not killing everyone you love."

Bigfoot said, "Whaaaaaaat?"

"I'm certain you heard me. You seem to have exceptional hearing capabilities. But just for the sake of performance, I said, 'I will kill everyone you love if you don't give me a sample of your blood.' I have tried for years to get one from you. Even paid a certain Afghani psycho to obtain as much of it as he wanted. And we both know *that* didn't work out. There were several times I set up heists just to get a measly drop of your blood. The most recent involved you blowing up a city block. Bravo, by the way.

"Alas, you don't bleed easily. I'm tired of trying to steal DNA samples from government labs. Once you're in the forest, you're hard to track, according to the hunters I send after you whenever you leave your big log fortress. And just getting cameras in there while you were gone gave my tech guys the willies, enough that they didn't check the equipment, which of course led to that whiny camera you discovered. I haven't been able to find a single brave soul who would take you on, face-to-face. I emailed you years ago asking for some hair. You wrote a rather rude reply. But anyway, it's really blood I need. I spent years trying to legally obtain a sample, going so far as to purchase genetic labs as fronts—to no avail."

"Parrrrrrrrrrrrfait." Bigfoot tromped a slow circle in front of the bear habitat, searching the crowd. The man's words sank into him like a cold shadow and coated his heart in thick poison. The Sasquatch Hunter had been a hired hitman. Bigfoot would slowly kill Parfait when he found him.

"Oh so detective-like. Honestly, I'm weary of waiting for you to connect the dots. I thought you were smart. I guess you are, compared to *most* of the population. So, what will it be? Give some blood for science or watch me kill the people you love? If you go right now to the cargo receiving area and get into the trailer-truck I have waiting for you there, I'll have some blood taken, and I won't have to prove to you that I'm willing to do anything to get it."

"Fuuuuuuuuuuuck yooooooooooou!"

"I thought that would be your answer. Very well. Perhaps an example of how serious I am?"

Junie, who had been pacing along the fake creek just below Bigfoot, yelped. Blood splashed from just behind her front leg and spread across her tawny fur. A rifle report followed half-a-second later, and the little bear collapsed.

"Next time it will be a human child. You know the child I mean." The man ended the call.

Another shot rang out. A bullet zinged off the pavement between the brother bears, who had stopped wrestling to stare at their crumpled sister.

Bigfoot bolted toward the source of the gunfire. "Ruuuuuuuuuuuuuuun!"

Yet another shot. Bigfoot didn't stop to see if it had connected. The shooter was on the hill above the zoo, hidden in the trees. Bigfoot jumped over scattering people and leapt the fence. He followed the smell of a sweaty man and gunpowder.

Footprints were in the soft soil near a thick pine tree and a few trampled fern. No ejected cartridges. The shooter was a pro. He'd gone back down the path toward the rose garden. Bigfoot knew he'd already faded in with the rest of the park visitors, and could have even reached a getaway car.

He looked down at the zoo. Park employees sealed off the bear habitat. Trainers surrounded Junie. Bigfoot heard the sirens of emergency vehicles coming up the hill. He picked up a boulder and tossed it toward the condos, hearing a crunch, pop, and the sound of several blaring car alarms.

Bigfoot jogged back to his monster truck and checked with the crows scrounging stuff from the parking lot. They still had nothing—except one told him he'd ripped his pants. They were more concerned about what went down at the zoo. Bigfoot told them everything, and they squawked the details to everyone within hearing distance.

He texted Lyle, which was a *bitch* for him to do: CAN'T MAKE DINNER. BEAR ASSASSINATION. GOTTA FIND SYD.

Chapter 13

Bigfoot sat in his truck, thinking. He was being targeted. It wasn't the first time, and not even the first time someone had tried to get some sort of bodily fluid from him. He'd not allowed it since he'd joined the Army. All the proper labs had samples. All the samples were still being examined. No one had divulged any sort of information they'd discovered, or even what they'd hoped to find.

Bigfoot thought about Syd's abduction and the rest of the missing persons. All the red-haired people. What was the connection? If Parfait had taken Syd to get to Bigfoot, then why take the others? Maybe Silver Linings wasn't involved in multiple disappearances. Perhaps Lance Parfait was behind Syd's abduction simply to blackmail Bigfoot. Bigfoot didn't like being blackmailed.

Three crows landed on the hood of his truck. He rolled down the window.

"A white van stole a teenage girl from a trailer park! A red-haired girl!"

"Yep, my brother saw it happen."

"His brother is a drunk."

"But not a blind drunk, he knows what he saw. And he followed the van just fine."

Bigfoot cleared his throat. The crows stopped yapping. "Thank you," he cawed. "Where did the van go?"

Bigfoot stopped at Vikki's and explained what was happening. She kissed him hard. "Come right back with Syd," she signed.

Bigfoot left his monster truck at his cabin. He took off his clothes and put his phone on the dresser—he wouldn't need it, especially since he was fairly certain it was being traced. He drank six root beers, grabbed his knife and a lighter and ran off into the forest.

An hour later, he sat behind a pine tree not far from his secret hideaway, peering through the dark with his Bigfoot night-vision at an old train tunnel where the crows had tracked the kidnappers. Two white vans were parked on the track-bed. A metal door sealed the mouth of the tunnel, which had been bored into a mountain. He saw cameras and security lights, but no fences or guards.

He decided to check the other end of the tunnel.

Bigfoot went over the ridge toward the south of the tunnel, making a mile-wide circle around it in case there were surveillance cameras, alarms, or traps. On the way, he smelled a campfire. Then he smelled Syd. Bigfoot stopped, turned into the wind and took huge nosefuls of air.

It was definitely Syd.

Bigfoot whispered as best he could, "Syyyyyyyyd?"

He walked until he was sure he was nearly on top of the fire, but he still couldn't see it. He hissed, "Syyyyyyyyyyd!"

Branches snapped, and a boy-sized creature vaulted into Bigfoot's arms.

Syd whispered in Bigfoot's ear, "I knew you'd come."

Syd had a lean-to shelter built into an overhanging rock with a functional fire pit, which included pine boughs weighted with rocks on the overhang to disperse the smoke and a high reflecting wall which served to hide the flames from every angle. Smart.

He explained what had happened. "They took Tate first. I guess he was already in that tunnel when they got me out of the van. I had my knife in my pocket. They didn't tie our hands or anything. I stabbed his shoulder, and he dropped me so fast. I just jumped over the side of the road and ran into a gully. I don't think anyone followed me. Couldn't leave Tate, so I've been hanging around." Syd tossed a stick on the fire. "Was hard without a knife."

Bigfoot signed, "Why did you get in their van?"

"I knew something was weird with it. They stopped and told us they had concert tickets. I was tellin' Tate, 'Let's leave,' when the side-door opened, and two guys grabbed us. Then they put rags on our faces. Fuckin' chloroform, man. Like in the *movies*!"

"What have you been eating?"

Syd smiled. "Well, I'm happy it's not winter, yet. Watercress, berries, birch spaghetti, worms, fish, a duck… There's plenty around."

Bigfoot squatted at the fire. He saw the boy had made a knife and an axe with sticks and stones. "Good job," he signed.

"Thanks. So, you're here to save Tate?"

Bigfoot nodded. "And hopefully others. Have you seen the vans come and go?"

"Yeah, but, really, I've been pretty scared. I didn't want to try to follow the road. I hear plenty of traffic coming up and down. And I'm not sure where I am. And you always told me to stay put if I was lost. I knew when you found out what happened, you'd come for us."

Bigfoot smiled. He signed, "I wish I'd have brought a sleeping bag. I had no idea you'd be on your own in the forest."

Syd said, "I have leaves, grass, pine boughs. I'm fine. You could maybe sleep beside me for the rest of the night."

Bigfoot curled up around Syd. The next day he would break down that metal door. As Bigfoot drifted to sleep, he wished he could tell Vikki that Syd was okay.

He dreamed that he was among hundreds of his people. They danced and swung from tree branches. They welcomed him, over and over again. The sun shone on ferns and flowers. There were piles of food. Water reflected the sky and trees and hair of all the dancing Bigfoots. Vikki floated down the river on a raft made of waving otters. She was naked. Her hair was dyed red.

Twenty crows chirped their greetings when Bigfoot woke. They had gathered in the trees around the camp. Bigfoot felt happy. He let Syd sleep for an hour longer as he gathered breakfast. Then he told him the plan.

Chapter 14

Bigfoot drew a map in the dirt to show Syd how to get home. It entailed about ten miles worth of walking through the forest, but he knew the kid could do it, and probably in half a day. Bigfoot gave Syd his knife and lighter. "Get my phone, call Lyle and let him know about the train tunnel and the kidnapped people."

He waited an hour after Syd left before going to the tunnel.

From the treeline above the road, Bigfoot smashed the cameras with rocks. Automated machine guns dropped from holes above the cameras. Bigfoot was glad to be in the trees. Bullets plowed the road into jagged furrows. He smashed the guns with rocks, too.

He jumped down to the road and tore the front wheels off both vans. He ripped out their engines and tossed everything into the ravine below the track bed. Crows gathered to watch and gather shiny bits of broken van.

"Shiny things everywhere!"

"Smashing vans!"

"Bigfoot rules!"

He bashed through the metal door to the tunnel.

Inside, it was dimly lit. Bigfoot stomped into the wide, rocky hall. Guns fired from both sides of the tunnel. Bigfoot threw rocks at them. He heard grunts and realized that people held these guns. He ran toward the shooters. One resumed firing. Bigfoot kicked aside the boulder that the gunman used as a shield, snatched the rifle out his hand and swept his feet when he tried to run.

The man landed with a thud and a gasp.

Bigfoot saw his assailant was dressed in black combat gear: Kevlar vest strapped with grenades, ammo and a gas mask. Three pistols, several knives, new boots. The man pulled a pistol. Bigfoot smacked it out of his hand, which snapped the dude's wrist. He yelped, but didn't scream.

Bigfoot lifted him by his vest. The man jerked in Bigfoot's grip as rounds tore through his body and sprayed the rock wall with gore. Bigfoot dropped the dead guy and jumped at the shooter across the tunnel. He clubbed him as he came down, breaking the man's neck.

A creaking sound reverberated through the tunnel. A blast-door slammed down across its entrance.

Shit. Bigfoot pounded against the door. It barely dented. He tried pulling the rock wall away from its edge, but found that the door was buried deep into the mountain. He growled as dust settled.

More shooters took aim at him from down the tunnel. Bullets sparked when they hit the metal door. Bigfoot spun around and roared. He rushed the shooters.

An attacker had the sense to throw a grenade. Bigfoot caught it and tossed it back. The subsequent explosion took out a few enemies, and Bigfoot arrived at the line of fire at that moment to pull the arms from two shooters and kick their knees and thighs into gristly, shattered skewers.

Three more attackers charged him. Their pistols blazed. A bullet zinged off Bigfoot's forehead. Pissed, he swung his fist wide and divorced the first attacker's head from his body. His swing continued, decapitating the next closest man. He slammed the second severed head into the third attacker, crushing his skull with it. Bigfoot punched into the man's chest as he fell, grabbed his spine and pulled four vertebrae and a squirming rope of nerve through the hole in his ribcage. He dropped the grizzled body.

One person tried to crawl into the shadows. Bigfoot picked up a pistol and threw it at the shuffling, scratching sounds. *Thock!* The man shuffled no more. He gurgled, but that was okay.

Bigfoot flung goop from his hands. Dust settled.

He continued down the tunnel, past a parked white van. It was empty.

Two steps later, Bigfoot smelled explosives.

He trotted back to the bodies and grabbed a few heads, some appendages and a couple of torsos. He ducked behind the van and bowled a head down the tunnel. A landmine exploded, choking the air with dust and peppering the walls and van with shrapnel and rock. Bigfoot tossed more body parts. Six other mines blew.

Damn, Bigfoot thought. He held his arms over his face and breathed through his hair.

He followed the trail of exploded landmines when he could see again.

It seemed these kidnappers were combat-trained. He was almost certain he'd stumbled into some sort of human trafficking organization that was apparently into redheads. Bigfoot hoped that Syd alerted Lyle soon.

Tossing a torso ahead of him, Bigfoot came to a tunnel connecting from the left that led deeper into the mountain. It was brightly lit, and its walls had been carved or tiled with native rock—smooth and uniform, nothing like the jagged train tunnel.

Bigfoot stepped into the passageway. Electrified cable netting snapped him off his feet, gathered him into a dangling bundle from the high ceiling and zapped him into unconsciousness.

Chapter 15

A light blazed into Bigfoot's eyes when he woke. He was strapped to a thick metal table. He heaved against the chains wrapped around his arms, legs, neck, torso and head.

"Kevlar and diamond woven titanium," said Parfait's snobby voice. "I wish it were your kryptonite or whatnot, but I finally found something that incapacitates you, so I'm happy."

Bigfoot snarled and strained. The table bent under him, loosening the chains slightly.

A man's head came into view. It blocked out the light. "This is my secret lair." He laughed. "Raise the table."

With a rattle and groan, the table lifted Bigfoot upright.

He looked down at Lance Parfait. He was a handsome guy, really. Classic clothing, peppery medium-cut hair, a scruffy beard on a square jaw. Bright eyes.

Several other men were in the large, open room. Most looked like thugs and mercenaries. All had weapons—a couple were big enough to do some damage.

Bigfoot growled.

"I have some business to take care of. I just wanted to be here when you woke. We're going to knock you unconscious again and move you to a more secure location. I'll speak with you there tomorrow. Cheers, Mr. Bigfoot."

Bigfoot flexed his arms and legs. The table crumpled around him, and he slid until his feet hit the floor. He twisted the table off its base. Electricity popped and wires smoked as Bigfoot roared and slipped farther out of the loosened chains.

"Oh dear!" yelled Lance Parfait, running to the exit.

The thugs opened fire. Bullets zinged off the table bottom and into the far wall. Glass shattered. Concrete ricocheted.

"Don't shoot him!" shouted Parfait. "Tranquilizers!"

Heaving the table, Bigfoot rushed backward toward the scattering men. He shoved when he felt the table leg connect with one of the goons. At that moment, two explosions rocked Bigfoot off his feet. Clouds billowed as he crashed into the wall. Tranquilizing gas filled the air.

Bigfoot and three of the men collapsed. The others wore gas masks. They slid Bigfoot from his chains and dragged him slowly out of the room as he fell into deep, black sleep.

Bigfoot woke in a small cell. The walls were solid rock. The door was thick and squat. After repeated attempts, he decided it would not break. Bigfoot howled. His head hurt.

"Bigfoot?" It was Tate. His voice came from down a rocky hall.

"Taaaaaate."

"It *is* you!"

Then there were other young voices.

"Bigfoot Cop?"

"Get us out!"

"Bigfoot!"

"Tate knows Bigfoot?"

Bigfoot snarled. He looked out of the slot in the middle of the cell door and saw the edge of another door down the hall.

Everyone quieted.

Tate said, "Bigfoot, can you get us out?"

"Tryyyyying," he said.

"You'll have to try harder." Lance Parfait came into view through the door slot. "Get the boy," he told a thug. "And another one."

The man returned with Tate and another red-haired boy. He held a gun to Tate's head and gripped the other by the neck.

Tate shook and cried, pleading for help with his big blue eyes. The other boy writhed and whined.

Parfait bent to look through the slot and said, "This is Philip. He's going to stay in the big cell down there with Tate and a few of the other kids. If you so much as flinch to shake a fly from your hirsute hide, he will first shoot this one," he pointed to Tate, "and then the rest. How many would you say there are in the cell, Philip? Thirty or so?"

Tate sobbed.

Bigfoot growled.

"Philip?" Parfait put his fingers in his ears.

Philip turned the gun away from Tate. He shot the other boy in the head. The crack of the gun echoed off the walls. Blood, brains, and bits of skin and skull sprayed the cell door and misted through the slot.

Bigfoot roared.

Tate collapsed alongside the boy's body.

Lance Parfait laughed softly into his hand. "Agreed?"

Bigfoot narrowed his eyes and nodded slowly.

Philip left, dragging Tate down the hall.

"Open it," said Parfait.

The cell door swished open. Bigfoot ducked into the hallway, stepping over the boy's remains and staring down his captor. He was tempted to squeeze Parfait's head from his neck, but a door clanged behind him, and Philip told prisoners to back up.

Bigfoot saw other rooms, some barred like jail cells, others with doors like the one from the room where he'd been. He counted at least a hundred people. Most likely all the missing persons cases he'd investigated could be numbered among them.

Parfait smiled. He motioned for Bigfoot to walk ahead of him. "After you, my fine furry friend."

Four men led Bigfoot down the hall. Six followed, and Lance Parfait brought up the rear. All the men wore gasmasks and were armed with weaponry that could knock Bigfoot down quickly enough. He let them take him where they were going. Deeper into the mountain.

Chapter 16

The men opened a door at the end of the corridor. A slight breeze blew through Bigfoot's hair. Negative air pressure.

"Please," said Parfait.

Bigfoot entered a vast, circular room. Its floor and ceiling were lit with a soft lavender glow. The ceiling was high enough to be thick with cloudy darkness.

He noticed carvings on the walls—carvings of his people.

The door whooshed closed.

Thugs encircled him, guns and rocket launchers raised. He looked down at Lance Parfait.

His little captor swept his hand in an arc. "Welcome to one of the grandest constructions of all time."

A faceted crystal ball about the size of small storage shed floated in the center of the room. Soft purple light shone from inside it. The floor was sunken below the ball, with a circular bench cut into stone. Carvings on the floor surrounded the depression. What looked like an astrological calendar, or a representation of a solar system, delineated in spiral grids. Lights were set in the floor in rings and spirals.

Bigfoot looked closer at the wall reliefs. It was as if someone had recorded his dreams. People like him danced and held hands, swung from tree branches, played drums made from logs, drank from mossy fountains and practiced

Nature Magick in all its forms. The light from the crystal made them sparkle and glow.

He returned his attention to Lance Parfait.

"Let me give you a little background, Bigfoot, though I know you've read my book." He waved at the circle of men. "Boys, why don't you guard the door or something? Maybe someone can bring us coffee. The big guy here isn't going to do anything that would cause harm to all those kids down the hall."

The men dispersed.

Lance walked away from the floating crystal ball. "Come have a seat over here."

More rock benches, sized for Bigfoot, surrounded a fountain. He sat in one.

Parfait paced around the fountain, gesturing with his hands as he spoke. "Not many people know about this place. It is older than most every ruin discovered on the planet. Bigfoot, would you believe that these walls were carved a hundred and thirty thousand years ago? Of course you would. Your people built it."

Bigfoot's expression telegraphed his ignorance to Parfait.

"Oh. So you *didn't* know. Then this lesson will take a bit longer."

The door whooshed open, and a thug pushed a coffee cart to them. Parfait told him to leave it.

He said to Bigfoot, "Do you take it black? Oh. There're no big mugs." He called toward the door. "Bring a Bigfoot-sized mug!" He poured himself a cup.

The same man returned with a huge glass mug in both hands. Bigfoot took it and filled it. It was great coffee. The best he'd ever had. He took his seat, trying not to be impressed.

Lance said, "It's Kopi Luwak. Harvested after processing by the civet cat. I drink no other coffee."

Bigfoot looked around as he drank. The carvings on the wall near the fountain showed his people in autumn: making love; harvesting; hewing stone; playing music; faceting gems and leaping over waterfalls. He also noticed that there were too many men in the chamber for him to break the little dickhead in half and make a dash for the kids.

"So, Bigfoot. You *do* know you're a Neanderthal, correct?"

Bigfoot did not know that.

Parfait said, "I figured you knew. Hmm. I guess you can't read the language, either."

He shook his head.

"Okay. Well. Let me tell you a bit about your heritage and how it fits in with my life pursuit. I am about to change the world, Bigfoot. Make it better. Cleaner, nicer, more... ordered. And you're going to help me. That's why we're here." Lance sipped his coffee.

Bigfoot wondered how long this windbag would talk before getting to the point. Hopefully long enough for another cup of coffee. He liked the big mug and decided to take it with him, unless he used it to brain Parfait. Then maybe still.

"This is Mission Control. This is the hub. And it's my new home. Oh, the work I've had done. I've quite the swank inner-mountain hideaway. You should see my *pool*. Anyway, that's getting way ahead of the story, of which you'll hear the abbreviated version because I'm quite ready to get things going here." Parfait refilled his coffee cup and motioned for Bigfoot to do the same.

Bigfoot did.

Lance strolled around the fountain, drinking coffee with his pinky lifted off the mug. "Neanderthal. How deliciously misunderstood your people are. Thought extinct by most of the world—only fringe weirdos and pseudo-scientists disagree. Even the conspiracy theorists and Bigfoot hunters consider you barely above the order of apes. But not me. Since an experience I had as a teen, I have quested to find your people and, due to my unique education and discoveries, prove who you really are."

Bigfoot raised his shaggy eyebrows.

"Yes," said Lance Parfait, "I met a Bigfoot family when I was a boy." He smiled. "They saved my life, actually. I stayed with them for three days until they took me to the highway. They healed my broken femur. In under an hour."

Bigfoot knew this was possible. He'd seen it done. It was part of the Forest Magick he'd learned before his real father had died. He was genuinely surprised that Parfait knew.

"I left it out of my autobiography. But you got to the part about my archeological discoveries, right?"

Bigfoot had read about Parfait's explorations in Bolivia, where he found what he thought was ancient writing but that no one else believed were words. He'd skimmed over most of that chapter because Parfait went on and on about how intelligent he was compared to everyone who had made fun of him. Bigfoot shrugged and held up his fingers in the international sign for, "a little bit of it because it was boring, and you're a blowhard idiot."

"Anyway, I saw that the Bigfoot spoke an intricate sign language. I realized that they were civilized. And so began my quest to learn from whence they came. Eventually, I discovered that Sasquatch are the remnants of the great Neanderthal civilization."

Bigfoot leaned closer to the little twat. He tilted his head in curiosity.

"Quite," said Parfait. "Ugh. You know, I really wish you knew all this. It's quite a bunch of stuff. I'm very tempted to not bother telling you. Or maybe I'll give you the blah, blah, blah version."

Bigfoot sat back. He sipped more coffee.

"Just kidding! I absolutely love that I get to tell *you* the story of *your* people. It proves just how far you've slipped. But we'll need more coffee. And sandwiches soon. Do you like tuna? Of course you don't. I have hummus for you." He clapped his hands.

When one of his men came over, Parfait explained what he needed from him and sent him away.

Bigfoot watched water fall into the fountain. He could smell that it came from deep within the mountain. It had seen many ages.

He thought about his people building such a place. He wondered why he'd never been told about it, even if he'd lived with his parents for such a short time. How could they not tell him such important information, along with lessons on how to disappear bodies—living and dead—or how to identify the smells of rain and what it meant for the near future. It was the most wondrous thing Bigfoot had ever known. It felt like home.

Chapter 17

Parfait said, "Okay. So, it turns out that around two hundred thousand years ago, after about twenty thousand years of *real* civilization, Neanderthals had developed technology far superior to our current tech, even the stuff *you* don't know about."

Bigfoot turned from the fountain. He faced the coffee-sipping twerp, who looked like a baby perched up on the Bigfoot-sized bench, swinging his tiny legs.

Little Lance arched his brows. "I know! Shocking isn't it?"

It sort of was shocking. But Bigfoot shrugged and sipped his coffee. It was getting cold.

"They became so advanced that they did stuff we would consider magic." Parfait watched Bigfoot closely. "And they lived like that for a long, *long* time."

Bigfoot finished his coffee.

The goon with the coffee cart returned.

Bigfoot refilled his mug. This time he put sugar in it.

Parfait tsked at that. He refilled his own mug, hopped up on the big bench and continued his story. "I began my investigation into this marvelous civilization while I was still among the names that held clout in academia. I was investigating the ruins of Puma Punku when I first stumbled onto it. Are you familiar?"

Bigfoot called out to animals with his mind, hoping something was inside the cave. Maybe even a scorpion, though they were typically selfish jerks that didn't do a damned thing for anyone.

None answered his call.

"They're spectacular. If the structures were reassembled, I would wager that they would rival this one. Anyway, there I was, examining the perfect angles of interlocking cuts on these monolithic stones when I noticed writing. Apparently, everyone considered it scarring or possible masonry measurements, but I recognized it for what it was.

"I spent four years at the site, gathering data and deciphering the ancient language—and really, it's not that complicated. There are only eighteen letters in the entire alphabet. However, I didn't have the complete codex at that point. From solar observations aligning with certain building sites, I determined the approximate age of the builders, which, even by conservative terms, coincided with the Neanderthal timeline."

Bigfoot watched as Parfait hopped off the bench and walked in a tight circle. "Anyway, I published my discoveries, showing each and every painstaking step of my investigation, pointing to areas across the globe that begged for research under this light, legends and evidence of who or what came before the Inca, the creators of monolithic sites like Stonehenge and Baalbek and the underwater cities of Japan and India. I was immediately blacklisted and my paper removed from circulation. My name was not only sullied; it was destroyed. But I was set free."

Bigfoot thought, *Who says sullied?*

Parfait said, "I went on a quest, researching the oldest legends of American indigenous cultures. When a seventy-thousand-year-old mastodon thighbone showed signs of 'butchering,' I realized that it was instead an incantation. And it nearly completed their alphabet for me. About that same time, I was led to a secret cave in the Grand Canyon." He refreshed his coffee.

Bigfoot suspected he did this for effect. The man hadn't taken a sip of it. Bigfoot drank more of his.

Lance climbed back up on the bench. "Is this boring you?"

Bigfoot shook his head. He refilled his mug as the little guy continued to talk.

"Twenty-seven mummified Neanderthals were stored there, kept secret for tens of thousands of years and only shown to me because I could speak the magic words to the current guardian. You should have seen that old Indian's face! Anyway, there they were, tucked deep in a warm, dry cave decorated with Neanderthal art and writing. And they looked just like you."

Bigfoot sat back down. It really was an interesting story. He was glad the little turd was able to tell him all of it before he pulled his guts out and stuffed them back down his throat.

"I confirmed that the mummies were Neanderthal through DNA sampling. Then I went to work on the language. I had the complete alphabet deciphered in a few months. The walls in the mummy room led me to this facility."

Bigfoot gave him a questioning look.

"Yes. *Facility* is the correct word. You see, Bigfoot, the writing on the walls around you explains that this mountain fortress is the hub of a network of beautifully sinister machines. When activated, it acts not only as a source of energy, but also the means to control the mind of every human on the planet!"

Suddenly, there was a muffled boom.

Bigfoot stood.

Bristling, the guards at the door aimed their mini-guns, grenade launchers and rockets at him. The door flew open. Additional goons poured into the room and surrounded the fountain.

Parfait slipped forward in his seat and swung his legs. "It's just the cops trying to blast their way inside. Your cavalry has arrived. But it won't get in." He slid off the bench and gulped his coffee. He put his mug on the cart before nodding at Bigfoot's. "Finished with that?"

Bigfoot drained his mug.

Lance strolled toward the crystal sphere. He pointed at it. "This is the key."

Bigfoot had figured that. He shrugged. He already missed having that big mug of coffee.

There was a louder boom. The floor shook.

Parfait chuckled and said, "I have tried for a very long time to activate this mountain. I finally realized that it will only accept Neanderthal DNA. I put a mummy in there, but apparently it has to be a *living* sample. At first I thought I was screwed, especially as my every attempt to obtain samples from you failed, not to mention all the laws about cloning—though I did plan on getting around them, if you'd only given me blood. Then I heard whispers of new discoveries about the human genome. I learned that there's plenty of Neanderthal in modern humans. Especially in redheads. I've been tracking down people with high percentages of the right genes and plugging them in. So far, it's killed every one of them. Just incinerates them. The ones who haven't tried yet have been working for me—building my lair." He smiled. "You really do need to see my pool."

Bigfoot, glancing around at the guards, growled and tensed.

"Oh, please. Be calm. There are billions of people. Why do *you* care, anyway? That's curious. I've always wondered about that."

Bigfoot stared at him.

"You know, I met you once, not long ago. During the only interview you gave about all the messiness with your wife. I stole a sample of your hair after you'd so colorfully declined my emailed request. I wanted to compare your hair side-by-side with some taken from the mummies. Of course, it's a match. Slightly different after these intervening years of change, but it's from the same stock."

The little man smiled humorlessly at Bigfoot's deepening glare. "Well. After trying a few people out on this thing, to no good end—but I do keep trying—I decided that I needed a full-blooded, living Neanderthal. I tried to find others like you, but since you came forward, finding even a footprint has become all but impossible. You were my only hope. Your celebrity, though not what it once was, made things difficult for me. So I came up with a more personal plan.

"When I saw you on those warehouse tapes, following the trail of your little friend, I knew I had you. If you didn't agree to give blood, I'd just make sure you found out I had the kid. It was a tad discouraging when the little shit jumped to his death in that canyon. But I figured as long as you didn't know I didn't have him here, you'd show. And having you here saves so much time versus cloning you and raising my own little Bigfoot."

Bigfoot made fists and showed his teeth.

Nervously, Lance cleared his throat. He motioned to the bench under the crystal sphere. "You are going to turn this machine on and make it do exactly what I tell you. If you do not, I will have Philip kill every single captive in that cell. If you still refuse, he'll move on to other rooms until there's no one left. If *that* doesn't work, we'll go get your new girlfriend."

There was yet another boom, closer this time. Moments later, something exploded just behind rhe door. Bigfoot looked toward it.

Lance shook his head. "They aren't getting in. Doesn't matter if they bring in the Air Force. Even if they make it into the tunnel, the interior is protected by Neanderthal technology. Stuff *I* can operate. And, anyway, they'll all be under my control soon. I'll let them in then." He smiled. "More workers."

Bigfoot squinted at the evil little douchebag. He didn't know if the machine would control people's minds or provide power. He didn't even know if it *was* a machine. Parfait could just be crazy. But he was certain he'd do something to Vikki. And to Syd when he discovered he was okay. Bigfoot scrutinized the well-armed men. He considered various options and their probable outcomes.

Parfait addressed one of the men. "Sam, open the door."

Air rushed out when the goon opened it. The rest of the men tightened their grips on weapons aimed at Bigfoot.

Parfait touched his ear. "Phillip. Shoot one."

A gunshot sounded. Children down the hall screamed.

Bigfoot yelled, "NOOOOOOOO!"

Lance motioned for Sam to close the door. "We can do this all day." He laughed. "Or all at once. Phillip really enjoys shooting people."

Bigfoot met the small man's eyes. He would kill Lance Parfait.

"I'm going to give you three minutes to get this machine up and running, and then Phillip is going to start wasting bullets on kids, one for every minute after three. Or maybe three for every thirty seconds thereafter. I haven't decided. At any rate, some lights or something better come on, and my cameras outside better show some *fucking action.* Understood?"

Chapter 18

Bigfoot sat under the crystal sphere, bathed in its lavender glow. Then, in a blink, he stood inside the floating gem. Bigfoot caught his balance and looked around. A purple haze filled the surrounding space.

From somewhere above him, a soft, female voice said, "Greetings, Whistler."

Bigfoot gasped. He thought, *What's going on here?*

The voice answered, "We've completed our interface. The neural link is established. You are Inside. Now, you need only think to communicate."

Inside what?

"The Seed. Whistler, I've detected that you're not here to enact the Plan, nor are you an agent of Flow. I've scanned your memories and learned how you gained access. This is most interesting. More interesting is the length of time I've been offline. The Plan has not been enacted."

What plan?

"Lance Parfait believes this facility to be a control center for the human race. It is indeed that. But not quite in the manner he has deduced. I believe he mistranslated our language."

Who are you?

"I am the Seed, the last technology of the People. I'm everything the People learned before and after their return to Nature. At least, until I was taken offline... Sixty-eight thousand, nine hundred and twenty-one years ago."

I don't understand any of this.

"It is obvious that you do not. Let me explain."

The lavender haze was replaced by a landscape. Bigfoot found himself on a hill, surrounded by giant cedars.

Below him, was a spectacular village built of rocks and trees. Neanderthal people walked between regal stone houses, climbed thick, leafy lattices of growing branch-walls into tall buildings, lounged in fern fields and tended to wild gardens, just like in his dreams.

"This is sixty-nine thousand, four hundred and fifteen years ago."

What am I supposed to see?

"The attack of homo-sapiens."

Hundreds of steely-eyed humans raced over the hill. Some appeared to run straight through Bigfoot as they rushed into the town, shooting balls of white fire from short staffs and thick bracelets. Burning and screaming, Neanderthals fell.

"Those are the People's weapons. From ancient times. The humans found a store of them."

What's happening?

"Humans are taking territory. They have decided, after not quite fifty years of cohabitation, they can do without the People. They consider the People foolish for giving up what they had learned. They do not understand."

Lightning blasted up from the earth, curling around each rock carving and latticed branch and encircling the city. It tore into and blew apart the humans who climbed through the village. The lightning burst outward in concentric circles, shattering trees and sweeping up fleeing men. Waves of plasma washed past Bigfoot. The air crackled. Nothing outside the People's enclave moved.

Neanderthals exited their homes, dragging human bodies with them.

"The People did not regress because they gave up

technology. They rejoined Nature. They needed nothing else."

The scene faded to the purple light.

Where did the humans come from? Why did they take territory?

"Theirs is a long and strange story. Just know that they arrived where the People lived, and though they were welcomed, they soon became a fast-breeding horde intent on dominating the Earth. They tried to pit themselves against Nature, though nothing truly goes against the order of the universe. Humans have caused a quandary. But that is because they are of dual Natures. I will not get into their story, but understand that parts of them are not of this Earth."

Suddenly, a forest scene opened around Bigfoot. He bent his knees to catch his balance. Before him, Neanderthals came and went from a tunnel in the mountain across a ravine. The scene changed quickly. He was inside the main chamber now, looking at the crystal sphere that hung in the air.

Bigfoot stumbled. *Could you not switch the scenes so fast, please?*

"Apologies."

Neanderthals hustled around the room, tapping on hand-held rectangles that appeared to be computers of some sort.

They're smaller than me.

"Since the Plan was not put into action, it is logical that Flow won the conflict. If that is the case, over the past seventy thousand years, you have been bred to be stronger and more congruent with Nature. Your physiology is Prime."

I see. So, the People returned to technology to battle the humans?

"Some did, yes. They began by awakening me. This mountain was my tomb. I had been laid to rest here tens of thousands of years before, with all the technological knowledge and history of the People."

A tomb. Bigfoot remembered what was happening in the room outside the Seed. He asked, *How long have we been connected?*

"Forty-seven seconds. You will perceive time as passing more slowly Outside rather than In."

I only have two minutes before they start killing kids.

"I will let you know when your time is nearly up."

I'm supposed to activate you.

"Perhaps you will."

I don't think so. Not if you're a weapon. Not if that man out there can use you to exert power over anyone else.

"You will decide what to do when I have explained the situation."

Bigfoot's perspective shifted at a reasonable speed. He felt less imbalanced.

"Note the screen on the wall."

A thick plate of glass to his left displayed a top-view of the mountain and surrounding area.

Beams of purple light shot from the mountain's peak and two other points near its top. The light spread out in three directions. The line from the peak was thicker than the others, and from it burst a plume of tiny lines like tree branches above the mountain. The other beams hit other mountains, hundreds of miles from each other. In turn, they emitted purple streams of light. The glow spread across the sky.

"This mountain is the central mechanism of a machine. Lance Parfait has that much correct. It is the control facility for a weapon designed to kill every human on Earth. Like a volcano, this mountain will erupt, but instead of ash or lava, it will spread a virus through the atmosphere constructed specifically to eradicate humans."

But it wasn't activated.

"Yes. I lack the data as to why. I can only assume that the Plan was thwarted."

The room faded from view, and Bigfoot was left in

empty lavender space. This time, he didn't lose his balance.

"The People had differing opinions concerning how to solve the human problem. Some said that all humans should be killed outright. Others reasoned that the invasion of this new species was the work of destiny."

Now, Bigfoot stood in a natural depression between two grassy hills that had been sculpted into a grotto, a steep amphitheater surrounded by carved granite. Neanderthal people filled semi-circular benches that faced a wide central stage on which a group of moderators sat. Bigfoot stood by the last row of benches. Fireflies danced in the air above the pink-cast hills. Soft lights embedded in the stonework glowed on the gathered Neanderthals. Bigfoot thought they were all so beautiful. He suddenly longed to be with his own kind.

The People before him voiced their opinions in a peaceful debate. They were speaking! And Bigfoot understood them.

We are stating that this is obviously Natural.

It is not in the People's nature to embrace extinction.

We are not calling for our extinction—though if Nature were to destroy the People, would that not be its course? We propose adapting to the inevitable change in the most natural and conscientious manner possible.

There are comparatively few of us already. The humans have populated much of the planet.

There are too many of them. They do not understand balance.

*Perhaps they **are** balance.*

The purple glow returned.

Bigfoot sat down.

"From these debates, a movement grew. An organization called Flow argued that the People's time as representatives of the highest order of civilization had reached its end. They devised a plan to retreat to the wilds and reduce their numbers through extreme selective breeding. They sought to seal the mountain for as long as Nature allowed and destroy any of their remaining constructions. In that way, the Earth might forget the People had ever existed."

But some of the People disagreed.

"An opposition called the Resurgents grew to counter Flow. They chose to use technology from ancient times. They awoke me, took control of my mountain nest and modified it to its current capability. Flow attacked the mountain many times. While the People fought each other, humans took advantage of the conflict."

Another scene surrounded Bigfoot.

Neanderthals warred in a forest clearing. Toppled and torn buildings smoldered in the distance. Bolts of plasma lit the smoky scene like flickering flashlights. A bloody Neanderthal swung a tree at another. Before the trunk connected, the intended target raised his right arm and, as though whipping a garden hose, strung a line of crackling lightning upward from the ground. The lightning surged into the tree, which exploded into burning hunks and splinters.

When the dust cleared, Bigfoot saw hundreds of humans swarm from the trees, screaming like howler monkeys. They shot Neanderthal weapons, swung obsidian swords and threw silent grenades that exploded in blue flashes and burned everything in a twenty-foot radius. Neanderthals fell around him. Blood and bits of hairy flesh splashed and clotted on the leaves and grass.

Enough!

Lavender space replaced the battle scene.

So what happened?

"Flow was successful in destroying most evidence of the People's civilization. This mountain remained under constant siege. However, the Plan was on schedule. It is curious that it was not enacted. My last memories are of a filed report on the loss of an eastern outpost, a seismic data stream from the far north, and a personal log from one of the scientists assigned to the project. They were preparing to execute the Plan. All systems are operational. Would you like me to activate the machine?"

What? To kill everyone?

"Only the humans, Whistler."

Kill the humans? I'm trying to save them. Some of them, at least. But then Bigfoot thought about his dreams. He thought about what the Seed had shown him. He thought about the humans' purposeful ignorance, their greed and desire to claim the world as their own. He thought about how they treated each other in their selfish pursuits, how animals were used and abused and how the brainwashing, power-mad elite had enslaved almost *everyone.*

"Whistler, there is activity in the control room."

What? How long have I been connected?

"Two minutes and three seconds."

The cavernous room replaced calm purple space. Bigfoot saw himself sitting in the depression under the Seed. It was disconcerting. So much so that he didn't immediately realize what was happening around him.

Chapter 19

The door, now dented and scorched, had been thrown open. Parfait's goons shot grenades and rockets at similarly dressed invaders, only these wore body armor, helmets, goggles and compact gasmasks. Bullets tore into the floor in front of Bigfoot's feet. Parfait ran straight at him.

Bigfoot took a step back and punched full-force at the little dickwad's face. His fist appeared to travel through Parfait. The momentum made Bigfoot stumble.

"This is but a display of the room, Whistler."

He turned in time to see the little villain slip through a hidden passage under the fountain's base. It slid closed over him. *Shit!*

Behind Bigfoot, the firefight sputtered to a few shots until there was only gasping, crying, moaning and the sound of knives opening throats. Bigfoot admired the quick work the invading force had made of Parfait's gang. He figured they were a special military unit. Lyle had called in the Big Guns. Bigfoot expected his partner to saunter into the room at any moment, now that it was all over. Bigfoot then noticed a soft, egg-shaped purple flow that filled the depression under the Seed.

What's this around me?

"I activated the shield when weapons were discharged. Nothing can harm us."

These guys are on my side. Get rid of the shield and disconnect me.

"I do not believe these humans are on your side, Whistler."

Men surrounded the Seed. They pointed their weapons at Bigfoot.

He walked through the display, closer to where he sat under the disco ball, ignoring the bodies his feet passed through. He'd grown accustomed to being in a projection. He thought he looked pretty cool sitting behind the wavering purple light. The room quaked. There was a distant boom.

How did they get in here? I hear them still trying to blow down the door.

"There are several entryways. The southern corridor appears to have been breached through a newly created tunnel."

A man in a tailored black suit approached the Seed from the charred doorway. He ordered the men to lower their weapons. Cupping his hands, he shouted, "Bigfoot! Can you hear me?"

Bigfoot said, "Yeeesssssssss." He recognized the man. He was the one from the park who'd pretended not to watch him and Lyle.

The Seed said, "He cannot hear you, but I can project your thoughts through the communications system."

In your voice?

"I can match your vocal patterns."

Okay. Do it.

"Done. Think and you shall speak."

Habitually, Bigfoot cleared his throat. He thought, *I can hear you.*

The smart-suited man spun to identify the source of Bigfoot's voice. Bigfoot freaked out a bit upon hearing himself speak a complete sentence.

He thought, *Seed, get me back to purple space.*

The man spun in a slow circle. "Excuse me?" he yelled.

His men glanced around the room, but maintained their positions, weapons ready.

The scene faded. Bigfoot returned to lavender light.
That was weird.

"In that case, rather than immerse you, I will simply project an image of the control room."

A floating glass computer screen replicated a view of the room from above and behind the Seed.

The man in the suit shouted, "What was weird? Is this really Bigfoot? I thought you couldn't talk."

You don't have to yell.

"Am I speaking to Bigfoot?"

You are.

"Right. Well, could you disconnect from that machine so that I may speak with you by more... traditional means?"

No.

The man paced in front of the force field. "Oookay. I'll just get to it, then. My name is... of no consequence to you. Let's just say that I represent *the* authority in this country."

Bigfoot thought, *Pshhh.*

"Yes. Perhaps. At any rate, we have been monitoring Lance Parfait and his schemes since he deciphered the Neanderthal alphabet. We learned of his plot to activate this device, and we know what it does. The rest of the story should be obvious to you."

Bigfoot regarded the mangled bodies that surrounded the man. *Yes,* he thought.

"Good. I'm glad you understand. But so we have things clear," the man spun another slow circle, waving jazz-hands in the air, "you are still going to activate this machine, but you won't place it under Lance Parfait's control. You will turn it over to me. You will do so now." He bowed curtly at Bigfoot.

This machine doesn't do what you think it does. If I turn it on, it will kill you.

The man flailed his arms and stamped his foot like a chicken scratching dirt. "Seriously, Bigfoot? Do you expect us to believe that?"

It's true.

The man in the suit laughed. "Really? I thought you were super-smart or something. So, do I actually need to threaten to kill everyone you love and make your life a living hell unless you cooperate? Do I need to get all *Lance Parfait* on your ass?" He did a karate chop.

Fuck you.

"Oh, Bigfoot. I imagined you might say that. I bet Bob here fifty bucks that you would. Pay up, Bob." He waggled his fingers until one of the men dug out his wallet and gave him a fifty. The man slid the money into his jacket pocket. He turned back to face the Seed. "I even said that it would be the cue for phase two of my coercion technique." He snapped his fingers.

About thirty children shuffled into the room. Two men herded them through the smoking entryway and positioned them in circle formation in front of the Seed. Bigfoot saw that Marianna girl. She was smiling. None of the other children were. They were shivering and crying and pleading to be let go.

No, thought Bigfoot.

"Fuck *you,* Bigfoot." The man pulled a pistol from his shoulder holster, put it to the head of the nearest child and fired. The bullet blew out the side of the boy's skull and struck a little girl who stood beside him.

Bigfoot gripped the glass display screen. *STOP!*

The children screamed and pushed backward against the men, who shoved and batted them with the butts of their rifles.

The man shot his pistol into the wall. "Silence!"

The kids stopped screaming. They huddled together, hugged and sobbed.

The man said to Bigfoot. "Understood?"

Understood. Seed, I don't want them to hear me.

The Seed said, "Now they cannot."

The man yelled, "Oh, I want to hear you, Bigfoot!"

Can you kill them?

"Yes," said the Seed.

"I said I want to hear you!" The man shot into the crowd of kids.

One crumpled. The rest tried to run away, but tripped over bodies and slipped on blood and brains. They clawed and stumbled over one another. Again, their captors smashed them with rifle butts.

Fists and teeth clenched, Bigfoot thought, *THEN KILL THEM!*

"Done."

The man shot at fleeing kids. "I'm going to fucking hear you or else! You—"

The floor slammed up and down suddenly, like the whole mountain had jumped. Everyone standing, running, or bending over to smack a child was thrown from their feet. The man's gun fired as his finger jerked reflexively.

The floor rose and fell again. The children and their captors were lifted into the air and dashed to the floor. Jaws and noses were broken. Wrists and necks snapped. Guns continued to spit fire and lead.

The floor beat like a piston.

A loud hum vibrated the control room.

Inside the purple space of the Seed, a large chair lifted Bigfoot off his feet as several glass displays formed a semi-circle in front of him. Each was lit with a different scene. In the center of the array was the screen that showed the control room.

The Seed said, "I have activated the machine."

Chapter 20

The humming sound rose in pitch and became a whine. Purple sparks lit the walls. On the floor, people screamed, convulsed and clutched their heads. One by one, their bodies began to pop. Blood shot from ears and noses. Eyeballs burst from faces. Heads and bellies exploded. The vibrating floor shook growing pools of gore into bubbling slush. Purple streaks of light raced in a circle around the room and arced through the ragged bodies. Bullets fired inside magazines. Grenades detonated. Metal and flesh erupted in twin geysers.

You're killing the kids!

"I am killing the humans, as you ordered. Check the other displays. Viral eruption in one minute, thirty seconds."

One screen showed a view of the mountain from a point far to the south. Near its summit, a rocky cliff-face began to slip away. Enormous boulders bounced down the slope, digging divots in the ground and ripping up acres of trees as they rolled. Clouds of pulverized wood and rock billowed at the base of the mountain.

A different display presented a closer view of the shedding cliff. A gigantic metal rectangle shone as rock fell away from it. The rectangle pushed itself out from the mountain until it protruded like a thick wing. Metal glowed. Violet lightning raced across its surface.

A display of the north side showed the top of the

mountain collapse. Rocks and trees tumbled inward, reducing the sharp peak to a caldera. Lightning rippled and danced on the new crater's rim.

Another metal rectangle emerged opposite the first. The top of the mountain became a shining dome of crackling, purple light. Dark flames flayed the mountain's skin. Molten rock flowed down its trembling slopes.

Bigfoot turned his attention to the screen that showed the tunnel entrance. Camouflaged soldiers ran from the blackened metal door. Paparazzi crouched behind law enforcement personnel. Vehicles bottlenecked on the dirt road and were smashed by rocks. The resulting debris blotted out Bigfoot's view of the scene.

The control room itself was a blur. Body parts, gun fragments, rocks and shredded clothing swirled in a vortex of burning light.

Bigfoot sat within the eye of this electric storm, transfixed by the weapon's power. He felt it in his body. Every hair stood on end.

"One minute, Whistler. Do you wish to abort?"

He realized he'd failed in his mission. Tate and the other children were part of the electric purple soup spinning around the control room. Lance Parfait had escaped. What was left for him now?

He pondered this deeply. Maybe it was his destiny to wipe humanity from the face of the Earth. Maybe the Plan had never been abandoned, only postponed. He considered all the pointless deaths he'd witnessed. Did a race capable of such acts deserve its position on Earth? Had his ancestors blundered when they failed to end humanity's reign before it could begin?

"Forty-five seconds until viral eruption. Again, Whistler, do you wish to abort?"

On the screen that displayed the train tunnel, Bigfoot saw Lyle hunkered down behind one of the squad cars.

He'd arrived to back him up—and had probably missed at least one dinner.

Bigfoot thought about Syd, who'd not only escaped being kidnapped, but had spent time alone in the wild without fear. He pictured him walking into his mother's house. He imagined Vikki's face as she saw him. Bigfoot remembered what it felt like to be held by Vikki. Then he thought about Lara and his dad.

"Fifteen seconds until viral eruption. Do you—"

Bigfoot thought the word as if it were a scream. *Abort!*

"Please confirm."

Confirmed. Stop the viral eruption. Stop the Plan. Don't kill all the stupid humans.

"Initiating reversal sequence. Shutting it down, Whistler."

On the displays, the crater stopped glowing. The metal rectangles retracted into the mountainsides. The ground no longer quaked. Swirling plasma in the control room spun itself out, burning up most of the blood, flesh and bone, leaving the room almost clean.

Bigfoot saw soldiers approach the tunnel entrance. Behind them, Lyle led a handful of detectives and uniformed cops toward the same door.

Thank you, Seed.

"I do what the People command. It is all in your hands. If you should ever wish to reenact the Plan, I will be ready."

I'll keep that in mind.

"Good. It has been a tremendous pleasure to speak with a Person and to catch a glimpse of the world again. I will seek to discover the circumstances that led to my deactivation. I suspect my memory was selectively wiped. Regardless, please return soon, Whistler. It has been lovely."

Well, it's been something. But I'll be back, Seed. Don't worry. I have more questions than you do. And I think I might bring some friends. You've inspired me.

"Perfect."

Hey, can you open that big door blocking the entrance?

"Done."

And disconnect me?

"Indeed. See you soon, Whistler."

See you, Seed.

National Guard troops crowded the tunnel. Bigfoot was happy to see that some of the captives had survived the ordeal and were being freed from their cells.

He savored the fresh air as he departed the mountain through swarms of police, soldiers, EMTs and other emergency responders. News people and paparazzi had already gathered beyond the dirt-coated squad cars. Uniformed officers held them behind yellow tape as helicopters flew circles above the mountain. The scene was so chaotic that he failed to notice Lyle behind him, struggling to catch up.

Bigfoot took a seat on the hillside below a canopy of trees.

Lyle plopped down beside him. Panting, he asked, "What the fuck, Big Guy?"

Bigfoot had no pen, so he just shrugged and clapped his partner on the shoulder.

Dust billowed from his partner's jacket. "Ow! Take it easy on these old bones! I've got a lot of fishing to do."

Bigfoot shook his head and rolled his eyes.

The Chief waddled up the hill. He was smoking mad. "Goddamnit! Those goddamn National Guard fellas are tellin' us we can't go in that goddamn mountain!"

Bigfoot stood and brushed the dust off his butt. Nodding, he started off toward the tunnel entrance.

"Wait!" shouted the chief.

When Bigfoot turned around, he found his badge thrust toward him in the chief's pudgy hand.

"You'll need this," he said, "to be official and all."

Bigfoot smiled.

The chief smiled back.

Bigfoot chased out the National Guard troops after he was sure they'd found all of the captives, staring down their commanding officer when he protested and hoisting two soldiers by their belts to toss them outside. Then he told the Seed to lock it down and keep humans out unless accompanied willingly by one of his kind.

The computer was more than happy to oblige.

Chapter 21

Bigfoot stood on the thick platform that connected the new tree houses he and Syd had built—with a little help from Lyle. He looked out over the trees at Mt. Hood in the distance.

"How many are coming?" Syd asked from behind him.

Bigfoot turned and signed, "All of them."

"How many is that?"

"Far fewer than there should be," he answered.

"A thousand?"

Bigfoot smiled. He realized it must be a big deal for the kid. Spending a week with every Person on the continent would be quite the experience for a human boy. He knew it was going to be quite the experience for *him*. Besides his mother, he'd only met two of his own kind in his entire life. "About that many," he signed.

Vikki emerged from one of the large buildings that clung to the old pines high above the forest floor. She walked across the wide platform to the metal fire-pit in its center, which was suspended from chains wrapped high in the treetops. Bigfoot had designed a series of Wookie homes, arranged in a circle with the platform connecting them. More were to be constructed. Soon, there'd be room for all of his new family to live.

Bigfoot and Syd joined Vikki. She warmed sage tea and handed Bigfoot the huge glass mug he'd taken from the mountain storeroom.

Below their cluster of tree houses, the Seed waited to enlighten the remaining People about their heritage and possible destinies. Bigfoot wondered where Nature would take them as Vikki snuggled into him and Syd tried to sound like an owl.

He was certain that it would be someplace right.

THE END

Kevin is a long-time believer in Bigfoot and other mysterious creatures. He's interested in ancient civilizations, especially those lost to history save for their inspiring monumental constructions. He spent last summer in the wilds of Oregon, searching for gemstones and keeping an eye out for the Big Guy. You can find him on Facebook. You might bump into him on top of a mountain, in the middle of a desert, or picking up a pizza from Sizzle Pie.

Bizarro Books

CATALOG   SPRING 2013

ERASERHEAD PRESS

Swallowdown Press

FUNGASM

LAZY FASCIST

Your major resource for the bizarro fiction genre:

WWW.BIZARROCENTRAL.COM

Introduce yourselves to the bizarro fiction genre and all of its authors with the Bizarro Starter Kit series. Each volume features short novels and short stories by ten of the leading bizarro authors, designed to give you a perfect sampling of the genre for only $10.

BB-0X1
"The Bizarro Starter Kit" (Orange)
Featuring D. Harlan Wilson, Carlton Mellick III, Jeremy Robert Johnson, Kevin L Donihe, Gina Ranalli, Andre Duza, Vincent W. Sakowski, Steve Beard, John Edward Lawson, and Bruce Taylor. **236 pages $10**

BB-0X2
"The Bizarro Starter Kit" (Blue)
Featuring Ray Fracalossy, Jeremy C. Shipp, Jordan Krall, Mykle Hansen, Andersen Prunty, Eckhard Gerdes, Bradley Sands, Steve Aylett, Christian TeBordo, and Tony Rauch. **244 pages $10**

BB-0X2
"The Bizarro Starter Kit" (Purple)
Featuring Russell Edson, Athena Villaverde, David Agranoff, Matthew Revert, Andrew Goldfarb, Jeff Burk, Garrett Cook, Kris Saknussemm, Cody Goodfellow, and Cameron Pierce **264 pages $10**

BB-001 **"The Kafka Effekt" D. Harlan Wilson** — A collection of forty-four irreal short stories loosely written in the vein of Franz Kafka, with more than a pinch of William S. Burroughs sprinkled on top. **211 pages $14**

BB-002 **"Satan Burger" Carlton Mellick III** — The cult novel that put Carlton Mellick III on the map ... Six punks get jobs at a fast food restaurant owned by the devil in a city violently overpopulated by surreal alien cultures. **236 pages $14**

BB-003 **"Some Things Are Better Left Unplugged" Vincent Sakwoski** — Join The Man and his Nemesis, the obese tabby, for a nightmare roller coaster ride into this postmodern fantasy. **152 pages $10**

BB-005 **"Razor Wire Pubic Hair" Carlton Mellick III** — A genderless humandildo is purchased by a razor dominatrix and brought into her nightmarish world of bizarre sex and mutilation. **176 pages $11**

BB-007 **"The Baby Jesus Butt Plug" Carlton Mellick III** — Using clones of the Baby Jesus for anal sex will be the hip sex fetish of the future. **92 pages $10**

BB-010 **"The Menstruating Mall" Carlton Mellick III** — "The Breakfast Club meets Chopping Mall as directed by David Lynch." - Brian Keene **212 pages $12**

BB-011 **"Angel Dust Apocalypse" Jeremy Robert Johnson** — Meth-heads, man-made monsters, and murderous Neo-Nazis. "Seriously amazing short stories..." - Chuck Palahniuk, author of Fight Club **184 pages $11**

BB-015 **"Foop!" Chris Genoa** — Strange happenings are going on at Dactyl, Inc, the world's first and only time travel tourism company.
"A surreal pie in the face!" - Christopher Moore **300 pages $14**

BB-032 **"Extinction Journals" Jeremy Robert Johnson** — An uncanny voyage across a newly nuclear America where one man must confront the problems associated with loneliness, insane dieties, radiation, love, and an ever-evolving cockroach suit with a mind of its own. **104 pages $10**

BB-037 **"The Haunted Vagina" Carlton Mellick III** — It's difficult to love a woman whose vagina is a gateway to the world of the dead. **132 pages $10**

BB-043 **"War Slut" Carlton Mellick III** — Part "1984," part "Waiting for Godot," and part action horror video game adaptation of John Carpenter's "The Thing." **116 pages $10**

BB-047 **"Sausagey Santa" Carlton Mellick III** — A bizarro Christmas tale featuring Santa as a piratey mutant with a body made of sausages. 124 pages $10

BB-048 **"Misadventures in a Thumbnail Universe" Vincent Sakowski** — Dive deep into the surreal and satirical realms of neo-classical Blender Fiction, filled with television shoes and flesh-filled skies. **120 pages $10**

BB-053 **"Ballad of a Slow Poisoner" Andrew Goldfarb** — Millford Mutterwurst sat down on a Tuesday to take his afternoon tea, and made the unpleasant discovery that his elbows were becoming flatter. **128 pages $10**

BB-055 **"Help! A Bear is Eating Me" Mykle Hansen** — The bizarro, heartwarming, magical tale of poor planning, hubris and severe blood loss... **150 pages $11**

BB-056 **"Piecemeal June" Jordan Krall** — A man falls in love with a living sex doll, but with love comes danger when her creator comes after her with crab-squid assassins. **90 pages $9**

BB-058 "The Overwhelming Urge" Andersen Prunty — A collection of bizarro tales by Andersen Prunty. **150 pages $11**

BB-059 "Adolf in Wonderland" Carlton Mellick III — A dreamlike adventure that takes a young descendant of Adolf Hitler's design and sends him down the rabbit hole into a world of imperfection and disorder. **180 pages $11**

BB-061 "Ultra Fuckers" Carlton Mellick III — Absurdist suburban horror about a couple who enter an upper middle class gated community but can't find their way out. **108 pages $9**

BB-062 "House of Houses" Kevin L. Donihe — An odd man wants to marry his house. Unfortunately, all of the houses in the world collapse at the same time in the Great House Holocaust. Now he must travel to House Heaven to find his departed fiancee. **172 pages $11**

BB-064 "Squid Pulp Blues" Jordan Krall — In these three bizarro-noir novellas, the reader is thrown into a world of murderers, drugs made from squid parts, deformed gun-toting veterans, and a mischievous apocalyptic donkey. **204 pages $12**

BB-065 "Jack and Mr. Grin" Andersen Prunty — "When Mr. Grin calls you can hear a smile in his voice. Not a warm and friendly smile, but the kind that seizes your spine in fear. You don't need to pay your phone bill to hear it. That smile is in every line of Prunty's prose." - Tom Bradley. **208 pages $12**

BB-066 "Cybernetrix" Carlton Mellick III — What would you do if your normal everyday world was slowly mutating into the video game world from Tron? **212 pages $12**

BB-072 "Zerostrata" Andersen Prunty — Hansel Nothing lives in a tree house, suffers from memory loss, has a very eccentric family, and falls in love with a woman who runs naked through the woods every night. **144 pages $11**

BB-073 "The Egg Man" Carlton Mellick III — It is a world where humans reproduce like insects. Children are the property of corporations, and having an enormous ten-foot brain implanted into your skull is a grotesque sexual fetish. Mellick's industrial urban dystopia is one of his darkest and grittiest to date. **184 pages $11**

BB-074 "Shark Hunting in Paradise Garden" Cameron Pierce — A group of strange humanoid religious fanatics travel back in time to the Garden of Eden to discover it is invested with hundreds of giant flying maneating sharks. **150 pages $10**

BB-075 "Apeshit" Carlton Mellick III - Friday the 13th meets Visitor Q. Six hipster teens go to a cabin in the woods inhabited by a deformed killer. An incredibly fucked-up parody of B-horror movies with a bizarro slant. **192 pages $12**

BB-076 "Fuckers of Everything on the Crazy Shitting Planet of the Vomit At smosphere" Mykle Hansen - Three bizarro satires. Monster Cocks, Journey to the Center of Agnes Cuddlebottom, and Crazy Shitting Planet. **228 pages $12**

BB-077 "The Kissing Bug" Daniel Scott Buck — In the tradition of Roald Dahl, Tim Burton, and Edward Gorey, comes this bizarro anti-war children's story about a bohemian conenose kissing bug who falls in love with a human woman. **116 pages $10**

BB-078 "MachoPoni" Lotus Rose — It's My Little Pony... *Bizarro* style! A long time ago Poniworld was split in two. On one side of the Jagged Line is the Pastel Kingdom, a magical land of music, parties, and positivity. On the other side of the Jagged Line is Dark Kingdom inhabited by an army of undead ponies. **148 pages $11**

BB-079 "The Faggiest Vampire" Carlton Mellick III — A Roald Dahl-esque children's story about two faggy vampires who partake in a mustache competition to find out which one is truly the faggiest. **104 pages $10**

BB-080 "Sky Tongues" Gina Ranalli — The autobiography of Sky Tongues, the biracial hermaphrodite actress with tongues for fingers. Follow her strange life story as she rises from freak to fame. **204 pages $12**

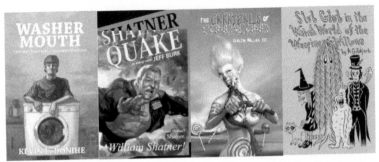

BB-081 **"Washer Mouth" Kevin L. Donihe** - A washing machine becomes human and pursues his dream of meeting his favorite soap opera star. **244 pages $11**

BB-082 **"Shatnerquake" Jeff Burk** - All of the characters ever played by William Shatner are suddenly sucked into our world. Their mission: hunt down and destroy the real William Shatner. **100 pages $10**

BB-083 **"The Cannibals of Candyland" Carlton Mellick III** - There exists a race of cannibals that are made of candy. They live in an underground world made out of candy. One man has dedicated his life to killing them all. **170 pages $11**

BB-084 **"Slub Glub in the Weird World of the Weeping Willows"** **Andrew Goldfarb** - The charming tale of a blue glob named Slub Glub who helps the weeping willows whose tears are flooding the earth. There are also hyenas, ghosts, and a voodoo priest **100 pages $10**

BB-085 **"Super Fetus" Adam Pepper** - Try to abort this fetus and he'll kick your ass! **104 pages $10**

BB-086 **"Fistful of Feet" Jordan Krall** - A bizarro tribute to spaghetti westerns, featuring Cthulhu-worshipping Indians, a woman with four feet, a crazed gunman who is obsessed with sucking on candy, Syphilis-ridden mutants, sexually transmitted tattoos, and a house devoted to the freakiest fetishes. **228 pages $12**

BB-087 **"Ass Goblins of Auschwitz" Cameron Pierce** - It's Monty Python meets Nazi exploitation in a surreal nightmare as can only be imagined by Bizarro author Cameron Pierce. **104 pages $10**

BB-088 **"Silent Weapons for Quiet Wars" Cody Goodfellow** - "This is high-end psychological surrealist horror meets bottom-feeding low-life crime in a techno-thrilling science fiction world full of Lovecraft and magic..." -John Skipp **212 pages $12**

BB-089 "Warrior Wolf Women of the Wasteland" Carlton Mellick III
— Road Warrior Werewolves versus McDonaldland Mutants...post-apocalyptic fiction has never been quite like this. **316 pages $13**

BB-091 "Super Giant Monster Time" Jeff Burk
— A tribute to choose your own adventures and Godzilla movies. Will you escape the giant monsters that are rampaging the fuck out of your city and shit? Or will you join the mob of alien-controlled punk rockers causing chaos in the streets? What happens next depends on you. **188 pages $12**

BB-092 "Perfect Union" Cody Goodfellow
— "Cronenberg's THE FLY on a grand scale: human/insect gene-spliced body horror, where the human hive politics are as shocking as the gore." -John Skipp. **272 pages $13**

BB-093 "Sunset with a Beard" Carlton Mellick III
— 14 stories of surreal science fiction. **200 pages $12**

BB-094 "My Fake War" Andersen Prunty
— The absurd tale of an unlikely soldier forced to fight a war that, quite possibly, does not exist. It's Rambo meets Waiting for Godot in this subversive satire of American values and the scope of the human imagination. **128 pages $11**

BB-095 "Lost in Cat Brain Land" Cameron Pierce
— Sad stories from a surreal world. A fascist mustache, the ghost of Franz Kafka, a desert inside a dead cat. Primordial entities mourn the death of their child. The desperate serve tea to mysterious creatures. A hopeless romantic falls in love with a pterodactyl. And much more. **152 pages $11**

BB-096 "The Kobold Wizard's Dildo of Enlightenment +2" Carlton Mellick III
— A Dungeons and Dragons parody about a group of people who learn they are only made up characters in an AD&D campaign and must find a way to resist their nerdy teenaged players and retarded dungeon master in order to survive. 232 **pages $12**

BB-098 "A Hundred Horrible Sorrows of Ogner Stump" Andrew Goldfarb
— Goldfarb's acclaimed comic series. A magical and weird journey into the horrors of everyday life. **164 pages $11**

BB-099 "Pickled Apocalypse of Pancake Island" Cameron Pierce—A demented fairy tale about a pickle, a pancake, and the apocalypse. **102 pages $8**

BB-100 "Slag Attack" Andersen Prunty— Slag Attack features four visceral, noir stories about the living, crawling apocalypse.A slag is what survivors are calling the slug-like maggots raining from the sky, burrowing inside people, and hollowing out their flesh and their sanity. **148 pages $11**

BB-101 "Slaughterhouse High" Robert Devereaux—A place where schools are built with secret passageways, rebellious teens get zippers installed in their mouths and genitals, and once a year, on that special night, one couple is slaughtered and the bits of their bodies are kept as souvenirs. **304 pages $13**

BB-102 "The Emerald Burrito of Oz" John Skipp & Marc Levinthal —OZ IS REAL! Magic is real! The gate is really in Kansas! And America is finally allowing Earth tourists to visit this weird-ass, mysterious land. But when Gene of Los Angeles heads off for summer vacation in the Emerald City, little does he know that a war is brewing...a war that could destroy both worlds. **280 pages $13**

BB-103 "The Vegan Revolution... with Zombies" David Agranoff — When there's no more meat in hell, the vegans will walk the earth. **160 pages $11**

BB-104 "The Flappy Parts" Kevin L Donihe—Poems about bunnies, LSD, and police abuse. You know, things that matter. 132 **pages $11**

BB-105 "Sorry I Ruined Your Orgy" Bradley Sands—Bizarro humorist Bradley Sands returns with one of the strangest, most hilarious collections of the year. **130 pages $11**

BB-106 "Mr. Magic Realism" Bruce Taylor—Like Golden Age science fiction comics written by Freud, Mr. Magic Realism is a strange, insightful adventure that spans the furthest reaches of the galaxy, exploring the hidden caverns in the hearts and minds of men, women, aliens, and biomechanical cats. **152 pages $11**

BB-107 "Zombies and Shit" Carlton Mellick III—"Battle Royale" meets "Return of the Living Dead." Mellick's bizarro tribute to the zombie genre. **308 pages $13**

BB-108 "The Cannibal's Guide to Ethical Living" Mykle Hansen—Over a five star French meal of fine wine, organic vegetables and human flesh, a lunatic delivers a witty, chilling, disturbingly sane argument in favor of eating the rich.. **184 pages $11**

BB-109 "Starfish Girl" Athena Villaverde—In a post-apocalyptic underwater dome society, a girl with a starfish growing from her head and an assassin with sea anenome hair are on the run from a gang of mutant fish men. **160 pages $11**

BB-110 "Lick Your Neighbor" Chris Genoa—Mutant ninjas, a talking whale, kung fu masters, maniacal pilgrims, and an alcoholic clown populate Chris Genoa's surreal, darkly comical and unnerving reimagining of the first Thanksgiving. **303 pages $13**

BB-111 "Night of the Assholes" Kevin L. Donihe—A plague of assholes is infecting the countryside. Normal everyday people are transforming into jerks, snobs, dicks, and douchebags. And they all have only one purpose: to make your life a living hell.. **192 pages $11**

BB-112 "Jimmy Plush, Teddy Bear Detective" Garrett Cook—Hardboiled cases of a private detective trapped within a teddy bear body. **180 pages $11**

BB-113 "The Deadheart Shelters" Forrest Armstrong—The hip hop lovechild of William Burroughs and Dali... **144 pages $11**

BB-114 "Eyeballs Growing All Over Me... Again" Tony Raugh—Absurd, surreal, playful, dream-like, whimsical, and a lot of fun to read. **144 pages $11**

BB-115 "Whargoul" Dave Brockie — From the killing grounds of Stalingrad to the death camps of the holocaust. From torture chambers in Iraq to race riots in the United States, the Whargoul was there, killing and raping. **244 pages $12**

BB-116 "By the Time We Leave Here, We'll Be Friends" J. David Osborne — A David Lynchian nightmare set in a Russian gulag, where its prisoners, guards, traitors, soldiers, lovers, and demons fight for survival and their own rapidly deteriorating humanity. **168 pages $11**

BB-117 "Christmas on Crack" edited by Carlton Mellick III — Perverted Christmas Tales for the whole family! . . . as long as every member of your family is over the age of 18. **168 pages $11**

BB-118 "Crab Town" Carlton Mellick III — Radiation fetishists, balloon people, mutant crabs, sail-bike road warriors, and a love affair between a woman and an H-Bomb. This is one mean asshole of a city. Welcome to Crab Town. **100 pages $8**

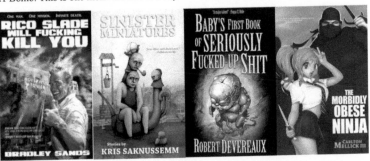

BB-119 "Rico Slade Will Fucking Kill You" Bradley Sands — Rico Slade is an action hero. Rico Slade can rip out a throat with his bare hands. Rico Slade's favorite food is the honey-roasted peanut. Rico Slade will fucking kill everyone. A novel. **122 pages $8**

BB-120 "Sinister Miniatures" Kris Saknussemm — The definitive collection of short fiction by Kris Saknussemm, confirming that he is one of the best, most daring writers of the weird to emerge in the twenty-first century. **180 pages $11**

BB-121 "Baby's First Book of Seriously Fucked up Shit" Robert Devereaux — Ten stories of the strange, the gross, and the just plain fucked up from one of the most original voices in horror. **176 pages $11**

BB-122 "The Morbidly Obese Ninja" Carlton Mellick III — These days, if you want to run a successful company . . . you're going to need a lot of ninjas. **92 pages $8**

BB-123 **"Abortion Arcade" Cameron Pierce** — An intoxicating blend of body horror and midnight movie madness, reminiscent of early David Lynch and the splatterpunks at their most sublime. **172 pages $11**

BB-124 **"Black Hole Blues" Patrick Wensink** — A hilarious double helix of country music and physics. **196 pages $11**

BB-125 **"Barbarian Beast Bitches of the Badlands" Carlton Mellick III** — Three prequels and sequels to *Warrior Wolf Women of the Wasteland*. **284 pages $13**

BB-126 **"The Traveling Dildo Salesman" Kevin L. Donihe** — A nightmare comedy about destiny, faith, and sex toys. Also featuring Donihe's most lurid and infamous short stories: *Milky Agitation, Two-Way Santa, The Helen Mower, Living Room Zombies,* and *Revenge of the Living Masturbation Rag.* **108 pages $8**

BB-127 **"Metamorphosis Blues" Bruce Taylor** — Enter a land of love beasts, intergalactic cowboys, and rock 'n roll. A land where Sears Catalogs are doorways to insanity and men keep mysterious black boxes. Welcome to the monstrous mind of Mr. Magic Realism. **136 pages $11**

BB-128 **"The Driver's Guide to Hitting Pedestrians" Andersen Prunty** — A pocket guide to the twenty-three most painful things in life, written by the most well-adjusted man in the universe. **108 pages $8**

BB-129 **"Island of the Super People" Kevin Shamel** — Four students and their anthropology professor journey to a remote island to study its indigenous population. But this is no ordinary native culture. They're super heroes and villains with flesh costumes and out-landish abilities like self-detonation, musical eyelashes, and microwave hands. **194 pages $11**

BB-130 **"Fantastic Orgy" Carlton Mellick III** — Shark Sex, mutant cats, and strange sexually transmitted diseases. Featuring the stories: *Candy-coated, Ear Cat, Fantastic Orgy, City Hobgoblins,* and *Porno in August.* **136 pages $9**

BB-131 "Cripple Wolf" Jeff Burk — Part man. Part wolf. 100% crippled. Also including *Punk Rock Nursing Home, Adrift with Space Badgers, Cook for Your Life, Just Another Day in the Park, Frosty and the Full Monty*, and *House of Cats*. **152 pages $10**

BB-132 "I Knocked Up Satan's Daughter" Carlton Mellick III — An adorable, violent, fantastical love story. A romantic comedy for the bizarro fiction reader. **152 pages $10**

BB-133 "A Town Called Suckhole" David W. Barbee — Far into the future, in the nuclear bowels of post-apocalyptic Dixie, there is a town. A town of derelict mobile homes, ancient junk, and mutant wildlife. A town of slack jawed rednecks who bask in the splendors of moonshine and mud boggin'. A town dedicated to the bloody and demented legacy of the Old South. A town called Suckhole. **144 pages $10**

BB-134 "Cthulhu Comes to the Vampire Kingdom" Cameron Pierce — What you'd get if H. P. Lovecraft wrote a Tim Burton animated film. **148 pages $11**

BB-135 "I am Genghis Cum" Violet LeVoit — From the savage Arctic tundra to post-partum mutations to your missing daughter's unmarked grave, join visionary madwoman Violet LeVoit in this non-stop eight-story onslaught of full-tilt Bizarro punk lit thrills. **124 pages $9**

BB-136 "Haunt" Laura Lee Bahr — A tripping-balls Los Angeles noir, where a mysterious dame drags you through a time-warping Bizarro hall of mirrors. **316 pages $13**

BB-137 "Amazing Stories of the Flying Spaghetti Monster" edited by Cameron Pierce — Like an all-spaghetti evening of Adult Swim, the Flying Spaghetti Monster will show you the many realms of His Noodly Appendage. Learn of those who worship him and the lives he touches in distant, mysterious ways. **228 pages $12**

BB-138 "Wave of Mutilation" Douglas Lain — A dream-pop exploration of modern architecture and the American identity, *Wave of Mutilation* is a Zen finger trap for the 21st century. **100 pages $8**

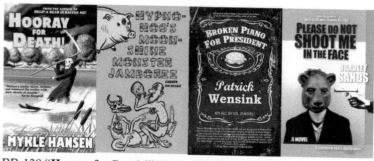

BB-139 "Hooray for Death!" Mykle Hansen — Famous Author Mykle Hansen draws unconventional humor from deaths tiny and large, and invites you to laugh while you can. **128 pages $10**

BB-140 "Hypno-hog's Moonshine Monster Jamboree" Andrew Goldfarb — Hicks, Hogs, Horror! Goldfarb is back with another strange illustrated tale of backwoods weirdness. **120 pages $9**

BB-141 "Broken Piano For President" Patrick Wensink — A comic masterpiece about the fast food industry, booze, and the necessity to choose happiness over work and security. **372 pages $15**

BB-142 "Please Do Not Shoot Me in the Face" Bradley Sands — A novel in three parts, *Please Do Not Shoot Me in the Face: A Novel*, is the story of one boy detective, the worst ninja in the world, and the great American fast food wars. It is a novel of loss, destruction, and--incredibly--genuine hope. **224 pages $12**

BB-143 "Santa Steps Out" Robert Devereaux — Sex, Death, and Santa Claus ... The ultimate erotic Christmas story is back. **294 pages $13**

BB-144 "Santa Conquers the Homophobes" Robert Devereaux — "I wish I could hope to ever attain one-thousandth the perversity of Robert Devereaux's toenail clippings." - Poppy Z. Brite **316 pages $13**

BB-145 "We Live Inside You" Jeremy Robert Johnson — "Jeremy Robert Johnson is dancing to a way different drummer. He loves language, he loves the edge, and he loves us people. These stories have range and style and wit. This is entertainment... and literature."- Jack Ketchum **188 pages $11**

BB-146 "Clockwork Girl" Athena Villaverde — Urban fairy tales for the weird girl in all of us. Like a combination of Francesca Lia Block, Charles de Lint, Kathe Koja, Tim Burton, and Hayao Miyazaki, her stories are cute, kinky, edgy, magical, provocative, and strange, full of poetic imagery and vicious sexuality. **160 pages $10**

BB-147 **"Armadillo Fists" Carlton Mellick III** — A weird-as-hell gangster story set in a world where people drive giant mechanical dinosaurs instead of cars. **168 pages $11**

BB-148 **"Gargoyle Girls of Spider Island" Cameron Pierce** — Four college seniors venture out into open waters for the tropical party weekend of a lifetime. Instead of a teenage sex fantasy, they find themselves in a nightmare of pirates, sharks, and sex-crazed monsters. **100 pages $8**

BB-149 **"The Handsome Squirm" by Carlton Mellick III** — Like Franz Kafka's *The Trial* meets an erotic body horror version of *The Blob*. **158 pages $11**

BB-150 **"Tentacle Death Trip" Jordan Krall** — It's *Death Race 2000* meets H. P. Lovecraft in bizarro author Jordan Krall's best and most suspenseful work to date. **224 pages $12**

BB-151 **"The Obese" Nick Antosca** — Like Alfred Hitchcock's *The Birds*... but with obese people. **108 pages $10**

BB-152 **"All-Monster Action!" Cody Goodfellow** — The world gave him a blank check and a demand: Create giant monsters to fight our wars. But Dr. Otaku was not satisfied with mere chaos and mass destruction.... **216 pages $12**

BB-153 **"Ugly Heaven" Carlton Mellick III** — Heaven is no longer a paradise. It was once a blissful utopia full of wonders far beyond human comprehension. But the afterlife is now in ruins. It has become an ugly, lonely wasteland populated by strange monstrous beasts, masturbating angels, and sad man-like beings wallowing in the remains of the once-great Kingdom of God. **106 pages $8**

BB-154 **"Space Walrus" Kevin L. Donihe** — Walter is supposed to go where no walrus has ever gone before, but all this astronaut walrus really wants is to take it easy on the intense training, escape the chimpanzee bullies, and win the love of his human trainer Dr. Stephanie. **160 pages $11**

BB-155 **"Unicorn Battle Squad" Kirsten Alene** — Mutant unicorns. A palace with a thousand human legs. The most powerful army on the planet. **192 pages $11**

BB-156 **"Kill Ball" Carlton Mellick III** — In a city where all humans live inside of plastic bubbles, exotic dancers are being murdered in the rubbery streets by a mysterious stalker known only as Kill Ball. **134 pages $10**

BB-157 **"Die You Doughnut Bastards" Cameron Pierce** — The bacon storm is rolling in. We hear the grease and sugar beat against the roof and windows. The doughnut people are attacking. We press close together, forgetting for a moment that we hate each other. **196 pages $11**

BB-158 **"Tumor Fruit" Carlton Mellick III** — Eight desperate castaways find themselves stranded on a mysterious deserted island. They are surrounded by poisonous blue plants and an ocean made of acid. Ravenous creatures lurk in the toxic jungle. The ghostly sound of crying babies can be heard on the wind. **310 pages $13**

BB-159 **"Thunderpussy" David W. Barbee** — When it comes to high-tech global espionage, only one man has the balls to save humanity from the world's most powerful bastards. He's Declan Magpie Bruce, Agent 00X. **136 pages $11**

BB-160 **"Papier Mâché Jesus" Kevin L. Donihe** — Donihe's surreal wit and beautiful mind-bending imagination is on full display with stories such as All Children Go to Hell, Happiness is a Warm Gun, and Swimming in Endless Night. **154 pages $11**

BB-161 **"Cuddly Holocaust" Carlton Mellick III** — The war between humans and toys has come to an end. The toys won. **172 pages $11**

BB-162 **"Hammer Wives" Carlton Mellick III** — Fish-eyed mutants, oceans of insects, and flesh-eating women with hammers for heads. Hammer Wives collects six of his most popular novelettes and short stories. **152 pages $10**

Lightning Source UK Ltd.
Milton Keynes UK
UKHW011310240222
399186UK00001B/312